THE WOLF
AND ME

RICHARD SCRIMGER

THE WOLF AND ME

ORCA BOOK PUBLISHERS

Library and Archives Canada Cataloguing in Publication

Scrimger, Richard, 1957-, author
The wolf and me / Richard Scrimger.
(The seven sequels)

Issued in print and electronic formats.
ISBN 978-1-4598-0531-6 (pbk.).--ISBN 978-1-4598-0532-3 (pdf).--
ISBN 978-1-4598-0533-0 (epub)

I. Title.
PS8587.C745W65 2014   jc813'.54   C2014-901549-6
C2014-901550-X

First published in the United States, 2014
Library of Congress Control Number: 2014935391

Summary: Bunny is kidnapped and held for ransom, and when he escapes, he is
farther away from home than he thinks and the only guidance he gets is from a wolf.

*Orca Book Publishers is dedicated to preserving the environment and has
printed this book on Forest Stewardship Council® certified paper.*

Orca Book Publishers gratefully acknowledges the support for its publishing
programs provided by the following agencies: the Government of Canada
through the Canada Book Fund and the Canada Council for the Arts,
and the Province of British Columbia through the BC Arts Council
and the Book Publishing Tax Credit.

Design by Chantal Gabriell
Cover photography by Shutterstock, iStock, Dreamstime and CG Textures
Author photo by Brendan Humber

ORCA BOOK PUBLISHERS
PO Box 5626, Stn. B
Victoria, BC Canada
V8R 6S4

ORCA BOOK PUBLISHERS
PO Box 468
Custer, WA USA
98240-0468

www.orcabook.com
Printed and bound in Canada.

17 16 15 14 • 4 3 2 1

*To my daughter, Thea, with love and thanks
for being herself.*

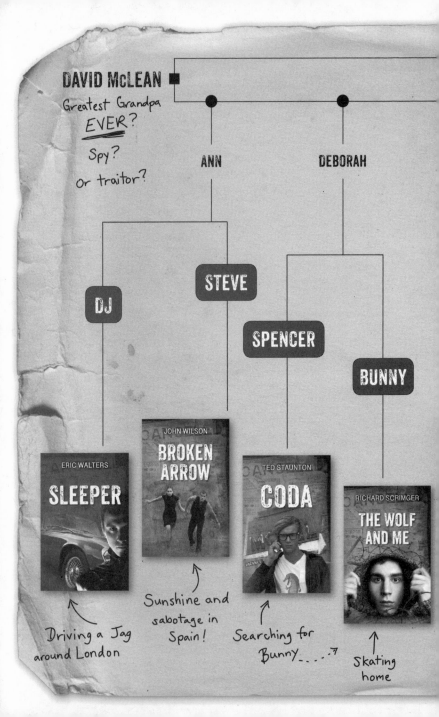

DAVID McLEAN ■

Greatest Grandpa
EVER?

Spy?

Or traitor?

ANN

DEBORAH

DJ

STEVE

SPENCER

BUNNY

ERIC WALTERS

SLEEPER

JOHN WILSON

BROKEN ARROW

TED STAUNTON

CODA

RICHARD SCRIMGER

THE WOLF AND ME

Driving a Jag
around London

Sunshine and
sabotage in
Spain!

Searching for
Bunny......

Skating
home

MELANIE COLE

VERA McLEAN

CHARLOTTE   VICTORIA   SUZANNE

WEBB

ADAM

RENNIE

SIGMUND BROUWER
TIN SOLDIER

SHANE PEACOCK
DOUBLE YOU

NORAH McCLINTOCK
FROM THE DEAD

On the road in
the Deep South

Channeling
James Bond

Nazi-hunting
in Detroit

**READ THE ORIGINAL
SEVEN (THE SERIES)**

www.seventheseries.com

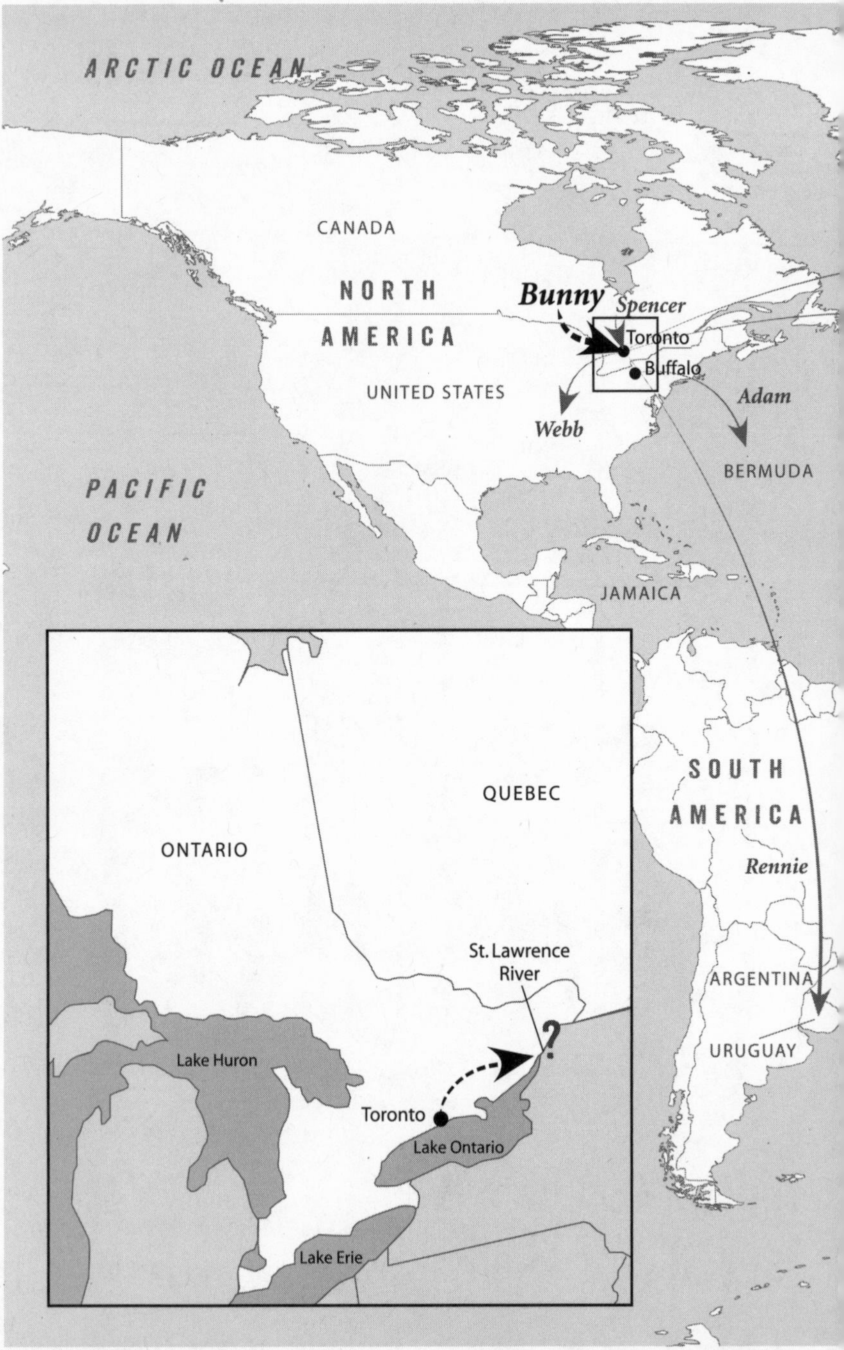

ARCTIC OCEAN
CANADA
NORTH
AMERICA
Bunny
Spencer
Toronto
Buffalo
UNITED STATES
Webb
Adam
BERMUDA
PACIFIC
OCEAN
JAMAICA
SOUTH
AMERICA
Rennie
ARGENTINA
URUGUAY
QUEBEC
ONTARIO
St. Lawrence
River
?
Lake Huron
Toronto
Lake Ontario
Lake Erie

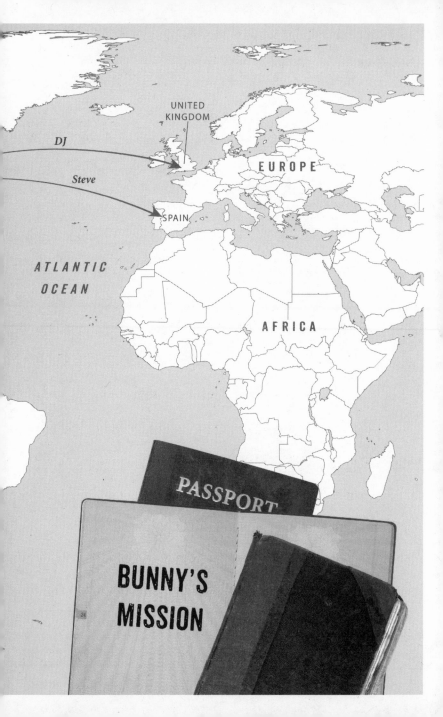

HELP. COME NOW.
IM IN TRUBBLE.

No thats not rite. I have to do the last word again. I rub it out. Im working on my spelling. Mr Wing says its way better than when I came to Creekside last summer. But Im still pretty bad.

TROUBLE.

I think about what else I shuld rite. I only have 1 small sheet of paper and there isnt room for much. The pencil is a stub—I hold it in my thum and 2 fingers. The room is cold and my breath makes puffy little clouds when I breath out.

BE CARE FULL. BAD GUYS WITH GUNS.

Now I need to rite where I am or how will they find me?

NEWMAN.

Thats the most important thing. The name on the male box. I saw it when I got here. I was feeling sick from the long drive in the dark and when the guys in the masks pulled me out of the trunk of the car I fell down on my hands and nees and started throwing up. The mask guys jumped out of the way and went *Eww.* When I finished throwing up I felt better. I took deep breaths and wiped away my swet. And thats when I saw the male box at the end of the drive. It was nite and the car lites were shining on it and there was the name in brite red letters on the gray metal of the male box. NEWMAN.

I want help to come to the rite place. I stand up on my bed and stare out my little window. Theres snow piled up aganest the bottom of the window cause I am in the basement. And theres bars running up and down the window like jail bars. I rite down what I can see thru the window past the bars and the piled up snow.

WOOD FENCE. WHITE BARN. THING THAT GOES ROUND.

You know those things. They point where the wind blows. This one is shaped like an arrow with a sun on top.

ROAD WITH 40 *SINE.*

That's the speed limit. The sine is past the fence down the road from the house. Not a lot of cars go by but when they do thats how fast they go. 40.

I get down from my bed and read over my note. Theres nothing else to put in. Pine trees and clouds and snow is the only other stuff I can see and that wont help anybody find me. Theres a bit of room at the bottom of the paper so I print my name.

BUNNY OTOOLE.

Thats me.

Its a pretty good note. Anyone reading it will know theres a guy named Bunny who needs help. They will look for a farm with a white barn belonging to Newman. If they are police they will come. And if they are not police they will go to the police.

I put the note in my pocket and wait for Vi. She is the nice 1 of the bad guys. There are 3 others or maybe more—its hard to say how many they are cause they all look the same when they wear masks. Vi doesnt wear a mask. Also she doesnt yell at me or push me around.

Thats how I know shes nice. She told me her name and said she wanted to help me. What we are doing is rong, she said. *WRONG*. Our cause is rite but this is wrong. Kid napping is wrong.

Is that what you are doing? I asked. Kid napping?

Yes she said.

And who are you kid napping?

You she said.

Oh rite I said.

That was this morning.

Last nite I didnt see her. I only saw the guys who took me out of the car. 2 of them. Pretty big guys with parkas and gloves and those ski masks with holes for the eyes. They dragged me out of the trunk and into the house and took off my skates witch I still had on from skating at city hall with my brother Spencer. The skate laces got into a not and one of the guys had to take off his gloves to undo them. He had white hands with dirty nails. The 2 guys dragged me down the hall and then pushed me down the stares. I was still feeling pretty bad. My head hurt and my legs didnt work rite. You know when your foot is asleep and you cant stand up? Like that only both feet. I fell all the way down the stares and lay at the bottom. The guys rumbled down after me and threw me into the room.

I didnt know what was going on. Thats normal for me. But this time I didnt have any idea at all. I mean nothing. I shivered all nite long.

In the morning an other guy came to see me so there were 3 guys in my room. The new guy was bigger than the other 2 and fat and his ski mask was red. They watched him. He didnt watch them. He was the boss.

I thot about standing up but I was feeling creeky. Also I thot that if I stood up the boss guy wuld nock me down and if I stayed sitting then he wuldnt. And if he nocked me over when I was sitting down then I wuldnt fall as far. Anyway I stayed down. He stood in front of me and asked questions about Mr Clean. At least thats what I thot he said.

Who? I asked.

I wasnt sure I herd rite. He talked English ok but with an axent. He missed some words and he said other ones kind of funny.

The guy on TV? I said. The bald guy?

I am not knowing if he is on TV said the boss. He waved his hands around when he talked. His voice made me want to clear my throat.

He wanted to know where he kept things.

Mr Clean? I said again to make sure. It really didnt make sense.

Yes Mr Clean he said. Where would Mr Clean keep things?

He pounded one hand into the other like it was a baseball glove. He turned and said something to the other 2 guys.

Yes Yes they said nodding. Mr Clean. Mr Clean.

They were all talking together.

It was cold in the basement. We wore parkas and our breaths made clouds.

I tried to remember the last time I saw Mr Clean on TV. He was bent over and he was rubbing a stove and making it shine. The woman with him was smiling. It was all pretty lame.

Hes got a bucket I said. He keeps stuff in there. Sponges and cleaning stuff.

They wernt interested in Mr Cleans bucket.

Somewhere else said the boss. Where does he keep papers?

I felt dum witch I am used to. I wished Spencer was there to xplain what they wanted. Hes smart and good at xplaining. He xplained what was going on at the cottage when we found the pictures and stuff. I didnt know why DJ was so xited until Spencer xplained to me.

I did my best here.

Mr Clean doesnt have any papers I said. Xept maybe a coop on. Do you mean a coop on? By 1 and get 1 free? I think he has those. What papers do you want?

And then he said—the boss guy said it and the others nodded there heads like they were saying uh huh—he said The Anthem. With capital letters like that—like it was important and I shuld no it. Like it ment something.

The Anthem.

I nodded. I no what the anthem is.

O Canada I said.

Cause that is our anthem. We had to learn the words in French and English in Grade 4. I remember some of them. *Carton brass a ton eh* something *Il say portay la craw*. Or something. Pretty cool. Something about a cross witch is not the same as in English. In English we stand on gard a lot.

OK I said. Mr Clean has the anthem and you want to know where he wuld keep it. Rite?

When you put it like that it sounds dum eh? It sounded dum when I said it. But the boss guy nodded his red mask and said Yes yes yes. And the other 2 guys nodded there black masks. And then the door opened and Vi came in.

This was the first time I saw her. She didnt have a mask. And she said my name.

Hi Bunny she said. Im Vi.

Hi I said. I stood up. It seemed like the rite thing to do. So there we all were standing up in the basement. It culd of been a party but there was no snacks and we all had our coats on.

I was hungry and I wanted to go to the bathroom. No wait—I wanted to go to the bathroom first.

Vi was tuff but pretty. You know. Like she wuld fite you and look good doing it. Her parka was fluffy.

Hows our hoss stage? she asked me.

What?

Thats what you are Bunny she said.

Oh I said.

I didnt know what a hoss stage was then. I do now.

Vi was the first 1 who called me by name. Later they all did but she was the first. And she talked normal. Like me I mean or Spencer or DJ or the Creekside guys. She didnt have an axent is what I am saying.

Has Bunny told us anything? Vi asked. Has he helped us?

Hes going to help us now said the big boss guy with the red mask. He is going to tell us where is the anthem. Arent you Bunny?

He said my name a bit different from her. Vi said Bunny like I do. He was more like Bun neee.

That is what we want said Vi. Where wuld your grampa keep the anthem?

What? I said. Is this about Grampa? My grampa?

Of course she said. Your grampa has our anthem and we want it back.

Oh I said.

David McLean is your grampa rite? she said.

Not any more I said. He dyed. But he was my grampa and that was his name.

The guys in the black masks were nodding and saying McLean McLean. I got it now. They wernt asking about Mr Clean. They didnt care about him or his bucket.

I xplained the mistake to the boss guy—mixing up Mr Clean and Grampa.

I didnt understand you I said.

He got mad and pushed me. My legs were still feeling num and I fell down hard and hurt my sholder.

Careful! said Vi.

You are stupid! he shouted at me.

I know—I shuld not of stood up I said.

GRAMPA.

So many things have happened to me because of
Grampa. When he dyed he gave me a task—a thing
to do. He had tasks for the other cousins 2. DJ went to
Africa to clime a mountain and Adam found a
painting and Steve had to go to Spain and like that.
Webb went up north to do something I didnt understand. My brother Spencer had to get a kiss from an
old lady actress witch was funny and also strange
because his task got mixed up with mine. My task was
to get a tatoo. It was a big deal for me. I got the tatoo
all by myself and all sorts of things happened because
of it. I am in a gang—sort of—who are pretty cool

guys thanks to Grampa and his tatoo. And Jade is my frend thanks to Grampa. These are good things that happend. Also I am in Creekside—witch is not good. We call it Creekside or Hall but it is jail. There are fences around it and you have to get a note from a PO befor you can go away and you have to be back when the note says.

A PO is a prole officer. Mine is named Roz.

Jail is not all bad. Benj and Lukas are cool and Mr Wing is an awe some teacher who likes my riting a lot.

But jail is mostly bad.

I am not in jail because of Grampa. He didnt send me there. But I got my tatoo for Grampa and I wuldnt be in jail if I didnt have the tatoo. Ive been away since befor Christmas. Roz said I had to be back by New Years or else Id be in trouble. I dont know how I can get back now Ive been kid napped so I gess I will be in trouble. More trouble I mean—Im in trouble now.

Heres what happened. Everybody in Creekside went home for the holidays xept for Benji who doesnt have any parents and Asa who lives far away. I didnt stay home for long tho. The day after Christmas mom left for a crews and dad flew out to BC to do weird camping stuff and me and Spencer drove up to Grampas cottage with our cousin DJ. There are 7 grandsons and a bunch of us got together up there to remember Grampa.

DJ is the oldest cousin. Hes like 18. Im 15 and Spencer is 16. Mom talked to Anty Ann who is DJs mom and they both said DJ culd look after us at the cottage. I didnt mind. DJ is bossy but OK. And he is just DJ after all. If he asked me to do something I didnt want to do I wuld say no.

So anyway there were 5 of us grandsons at the cottage—DJ Adam Webb Spencer and me. We were making a fire in the fire place when we found all this cool stuff—pass ports with Grampas picture on them and money from other places. Lots of money. And golf balls—I remember them. This stuff was secret. It came out of the wall. There was even a gun. I know because I fired it. I didnt think it wuld go off but it did. Bang. I was surprised.

They all got xited about the stuff we found. DJ and Adam and Webb did—and even Spencer did a bit. I didnt care. Grampa was dead. He culdnt use the pass ports any more or shoot the gun or play golf. They kept talking tho. They culdnt decide if Grampa was working for us or for them. I didnt say much.

I didnt want to spoil things by asking dum questions like—What work was Grampa doing? And—Who is us? Who is them?

Later Spencer xplained that the stuff we found in the wall was spy stuff. That was Grampas work.

Like James Bond I said.

Remember the picture in that movy? Spencer asked me. You said it was Grampa.

That was a spy movy?

Maybe.

Last time Spencer came to Creekside to visit me he showed me a home movy with a picture of Grampa in it. At least I thot it was Grampa. Spencer wasnt sure. He showed the picture to mom and dad a few days ago and they wernt sure ether. So Grampa was maybe a spy.

But I still didnt get about us and them. Whoever he was working for was us wasnt it? I asked Spencer.

It's about how much you trust Grampa he said.

We talked more about it on the way back to Toronto the next day. DJ was driving me and Spencer and he talked a lot. He had plans for finding out about Grampa. He was dropping us off on his way to the air port. I have to go to the air port he said. Thats the sort of guy DJ is. An air port guy.

I just wanted to go skating. Thats the kind of guy I am. And Spencer said OK. So DJ dropped us at city hall and we went skating. This was around dinner time. It was dark. I got some skates and zoomed around. I like skating. Spencer went to get some food and I was skating back ward and the next thing I new I had a bag on my head. I felt a pain in my side like somebody stabbing me. I yelled and then went to sleep and woke up in the trunk of a car at the Newman place feeling like blah.

Was it only yesterday?

THE MASK GUYS

wanted me to tell them about Grampa and papers but I didnt know much. The big boss in the red mask got mad.

Where does McLean keep papers? he shouted. Where is the anthem? Where?

He took a gun out of his pocket and started waving it around.

Talk! he shouted. Or I will shoot you!

I wuld of been scareder but I had to go to the bathroom. Its hard to be scared when you really have to pee.

Vi stepped in between the boss guy and me.

Let Bunny alone. He doesnt know anything she said.

She pushed him out of the way even tho he was much bigger than her.

The three mask guys went off and talked to each other. I didnt understand what they said but I herd the word Spencer.

Spencer is my brother I said.

So they started to ask me about Spencer.

Does he know where is the anthem? asked the boss.

I dont know I said.

Spencer is a smart guy. He doesnt always see stuff but he knows stuff. He didnt see Grampa in the video we looked at. Even tho it was clear to me.

I wanted to call him but I didnt have my phone. It was in my pocket when I was skating but I didnt have it now. Did Spencer know where I was? Probly not. Was he worried? Probly.

We will call Spencer the boss told me.

Can I talk to him? I asked.

No said the boss.

He left with the other 2 mask guys. It was only me and Vi.

Sorry Bunny she said.

Thats ok I said.

No it isnt. We shuld treat you better. I believe in our cause but I dont want to hurt you.

She was talking soft. Her eyes were big and wet like she was about to cry. Im sorry she said agane. What can I get you?

Uh I said.

Wuld you like something to eat?

Yes I said. But uh first—

I was hopping up and down.

Oh she said.

There was a black mask guy standing at the top of the basement stares. He nodded down to me. The bathroom was small and dusty. The stone floor was cold on my winter sock feet. I didnt care at all.

When I got back to my room Vi had a paper and pencil in her hand.

Rite a note she said. Put down what you know about what is going on and I will deliver it. Do you want to go to the police? I will take it to there. What we are doing is rong. I am on your side she said.

I didnt know what to say.

Trust me she said.

And she left.

That was a few minits ago. I wrote the note about what I culd see from my window—the barn and the speed limit sine—and now I am wating for Vi to come back so I can give it to her.

I CAN TAKE THIS TO THE POLICE SHE SAYS.

She is wearing a scarf now.

Sure I say. Or give it to somebody who can give it to the police.

I dont want you to get in trouble I say.

That is okay she says. I do not like what Lubor is doing to you. He is mean.

Who is Lubor? I say.

I dont know how to spell the name. It may be Lewbor or Luboar or something else. But Lubor is what it sounds like so that is how I am riting it.

Lubor is the boss of this sell says Vi. He is in charge of us.

Oh I say. Then I have to ask what she means.

What is a sell?

We are. All of us in the unit says Vi. Lubor is in charge. When he said we were going to Toronto to kid nap someone I thot we wuld be nice. I didnt know how mean we culd be she says.

She reads the note again and nods to her self.

Is this all you know Bunny? she says. Do you know where is the anthem? Where your grampa wuld keep it? In his house? In his bank?

No I say. Spencer mite know but I dont.

She puts the note in her pocket. I hate that Lubor she says.

He is the big guy in the red mask?

Yes Bunny. I am on your side not his. I will take this letter to the police. Wait for them, ok? Do not try to escape—I dont want you to get hurt.

OK I say.

Great she says. We are on the same side now.

And she leans over and gives me a kiss on the cheek. She smells nice.

Thats our secret she says.

And she goes.

Its cold in the basement but I am not cold.

I WAIT FOR THE POLICE ALL DAY.

They do not come. I think about good and bad and James Bond. Is he a good guy just because he is on our side? If he was on the other side wuld he still be a good guy? And what if *we* were on the other side? Wuld he be a bad guy even tho he is James Bond? I start to get confused and switch to thinking about Grampa. Was he bad or good? I gess it depends what side you are on.

Vi is good. She doesnt like Lubor and she kissed me. That's one way to tell if someone is good. If they kiss you.

I keep looking out the window to see if the police are coming. A truck goes by and a car—but not a police car. It slides sideways down the road. It is not going 40—more like 10. A mask guy comes down with a sandwich and some more water. He takes me to the bathroom.

1 time when I am looking out the window I see the guys in the black masks working behind the wood fence with shovels and you will never believe what they are doing. Go on gess.

They are getting ready to skate.

There is a rink inside the fence and they are cleaning it. It doesnt take them long. Soon they are skating. I see them bent over going fast and faster around the rink. One of them is a pretty good skater and the other is pretty bad. That is a way to tell them apart because other wise they are the same. There is just the 2 of them for a while and then 2 other guys come out. They dont have masks.

They play hockey for a bit. I see there sticks. When the puck goes over the bords they get it. One of them has boots on and the others have skates. Every body is breathing hard. I cant tell about the guys with masks but the guys without masks are smiling. Where ever these guys are from they like hockey.

I shiver in my blanket all nite long. In the morning the window is frosted over. I cant see anything. My breath is frosty. A mask guy takes me to the bathroom witch is so cold the tap doesnt work. Time passes slowly. Like it has big boots and can not lift its feet.

Vi comes in with breakfast—toast and jam and water like yesterday. She smiles at me.

I handed in the note she says. I didnt have a lot of time in town yesterday but I ran into the police station and gave it to them.

Great I say. So when are the police coming?

Soon she says. You wait here and you will be ok.

I wonder if she is going to kiss me again. The last person to kiss me was Jade. Its not like shes my girl frend but still. I wonder how old Vi is? Older than me but how much older? A black mask guy comes in and Vi goes away. Oh well.

The mask guy talks to me while I eat.

You are a boy from Canada he says. You have skates.

Uh huh I say.

I am thinking that rite now my rented skates are all I have. My boots are back at the city hall.

The guy talks some more. He tells me about himself. He is not from Canada. His home is a place that sounds like Pee and Vee. He asks if I have heard of some guy who plays hockey for Vancoover in the NHL. This player is from Pee and Vee he says. He is a hero there.

I have never heard of Pee and Vee. I do not know if it is a country or a city or what it is. I do not know the NHL player ether.

But you play hockey yes? the mask guy asks.

I nod. I am not bad. I am better than my brother and his frends. I like skating.

Wuld you—

He stops then goes on.

Wuld you play with us? he asks. There is a rink in the front yard. We wuld like to play with a Canadian player. Please play with us Bunny.

I dont know what to say. He sounds like an ok guy.

I gess so I say.

We shake hands. He tells me his name.

Bojan? I say. He shrugs. Maybe I am saying it rong. It is something like Bojan.

THE SUN IS DOWN BUT THERE IS STILL LITE IN THE SKY.

I am playing hockey with Bojan and the other mask guy whose name is Peter. I am on there team. Lubor the big boss is playing with 2 guys I dont know. The score is 4 to 4 or maybe 5 to 5. It is tyed.

Vi comes out and then goes back in. She is not a hockey fan. Or maybe she doesnt want to be with Lubor.

I skate hard. My blades are sharp. I am having fun—witch sounds stupid because after all these are my kid nappers. I am a hoss stage. But the only guy I dont like is Lubor and when you play a game with a bunch of people there is usually somebody you dont like.

Think about that.

There is some shoving and elbowing but nobody gets mad xept Lubor. One time I am over by the bords and he trys to cross check me. I duck and the stick goes over my head. I tell him to watch out. Shut up he says. There is a ring of white ice around the mouth of his red mask from where he is breathing. I pass to Peter behind my back and he scores. Lubor slams his stick down on the ice.

On the next rush one of the new guys has the puck. He has boots on and is sliding over the ice. His nose drips. He passes to Lubor but I get my stick out and stop the puck. Lubor charges at me like a bull going after Bugs Bunny. I duck at the last minit and Lubor goes flying over me and hits his head on the bords and lands on the ice and starts to bleed.

We stop playing and carry him inside. Lubor is out cold. The kitchen is the first room we come to and we lay him on the table.

When Vi sees him she starts to cry.

That is rite. She runs over and takes his head in her hands and kisses him. And then glares at me.

You did this she says.

What? I say.

27

You and Lubor hate each other she says.

She is crying and holding Lubor and calling his name and I am surprised as anything.

AS ANYTHING.

I say the first thing that comes to me.

Your the good cop I say.

Like in a police show you know? Theres a bad cop and a good cop. They seem different but they are working together. They are both cops. So Lubor is scaring me and Vi is kissing me but they both want the same thing. They want to know what I know about Grampa and the anthem.

I forget that Peter and Bojan and the others are there. It is just me and Vi and she is a lyer. She does not hate Lubor. She likes him. She has always liked him. She did not take my note to the police. She and I are not on the same side. She was lying to me all this time.

Wow I say. Wow I think.

I walk outside. Bojan comes with me. And so does the guy with the drippy nose. They are garding me. Bojan takes off his skates and puts his boots back on.

I breath in the fresh air. It is cold and clean winter air.

Vi is not on my side. The police are not coming to get me and bring me home. Wow.

I trusted her and I was rong.

There are no cars on the road. I can hear the nite sounds and the cold sounds—the crack of the ice and the wistle of the wind. I hop over to the rink and skate around while Bojan and the drippy nose guy watch. It is cold and the hi way lites show all the snow and ice that is packed and stacked and planked down. The drive way is coverd. So is the road. It is ice as far as I can see. A real Canadian winter seen.

I get an idea. Partly it is from knowing that the police are not coming. Partly it is from wanting to get back to Creekside and call Spencer who will be worryed. A lot of it is not wanting to be a hoss stage. I had some fun playing hockey but I am not having fun now and I do not want to help these people. My idea is to get away now. Bojan and the other guy are in boots. I am in skates. I can go faster than them. Lubor is sleeping. Vi cant catch me. Why not skate away rite now?

So I do. I hop over the bords and head for the drive. Bojan takes a minit to work out what is happening and then yells at me.

Bunny stop!

Bojan is sort of an ok guy. I can play hockey with him. But I dont want to be his prisoner. I skate down the drive and turn. The road is icy. I am going ok. A bit bumpy but ok. I skate past the 40 sine. I dont know what way I am going but it doesnt matter. I am going away from my prison and that is the rite way.

I am skating home.

THINGS GET UGLY
RITE AWAY.

I hear the car start up. Oh crap! I think. How can I skate faster than a car can drive? I call myself names. Stupid I think. Dummy. They are rite about you. You can not plan a head.

I look back over my sholder to see where the car is. And I start to laff. The ice is every where and the car is not going the way Bojan wants it to go. I watch it slide down the drive and across the road and into the ditch at the far side. The drippy nose guy has all ready slipped. He is lying on his back in the drive way.

Maybe I am smarter than I know.

My skates cut into the ice. I zoom along. The road bends to the rite and I follow the bend. I can not see the Newman place any more. There is lite in the sky to my left. And there are street lites every now and then. I pass another car in the ditch and then a truck in the ditch. No one is driving. I keep going. I can do this as long as I have to. I keep my eyes open for a place to stop and get help.

Skate skate skate.

The first place I pass has no lites on. Nether does the second. The places are far apart. There are fields in between. I am some where in the country. The third place is lit up but no one is home. I try the front door and the back but no one comes.

I wonder what I shuld do. The place has a clear patch of ice in the back with some snow piled up. I hop over the snow and skate across the open ice for something to do. I remember learning to skate. Dads arms around me. Mom telling him to let me go. Dad worrying about me falling. Mom saying so what every body falls.

My mom—tuff lady.

I get back on the road and keep skating. I pass another speed limit sine. It looks rong somehow.

And then I come to a salt truck. It is resting by the side of the road. I am so happy. I skate up to the door and wave my hands. The driver rolls down his window.

Help he says. A surprise since I was going to ask him for help.

What?

Im stuck he says. And my sell phone is out of power. Do you have a sell phone kid?

I shake my head.

Sorry.

Well can you go home and tell your mom or dad to call in? This stupid wether is killing me. Im supposed to get 40 miles of hi way salted and I am stuck in the ditch.

Sorry I say again.

You got the rite idea he says. Skates. Wish I had em.

Yah I say.

Go home kid he says rolling up the window.

Skate rite home. Thats what I want to do.

This guy is not going to save me. I skate away. I keep going until I come to my first cross street. Still no cars or walkers. Or skaters. Theres a sine that says *RICO CITY LIMIT* with an arrow pointing the way but I cant see a city. Or even a house. I have never heard of Rico Ontario. Not even on the wether report from CBC that they listen to at Creekside witch is how I have herd of Red Lake Pickle Lake Kenora and Rainy River.

I turn left to follow the arrow. I can skate faster than I can run. I bend over and put my hands on my nees to go even faster. Nothing but woods and stars for a while. The next place I come to has a lite on the porch and a car in the drive. I skate up the walk and ring the bell. I hear it like a voice in a dream. *Bing Bong.* No 1 comes out.

I put up my hands to cup my face and look thru the window beside the door. I can see into the living room. And there is the woman who lives here. She is in her house.

Only problem—she seems to be dead. O wait no. She gets up.

THE OLD LADYS LEGS
WORK LIKE MY BRAIN

—slow and not strait. She opens the door and peers up at me.

You are not God are you? she says.

What? I say.

I was having the most wonderful dream she says. God was showing me how the univers works and I was taking notes. And then the grate bell to end all time was ringing in my dream and it was the door bell.

I dont know what to say.

In my dream God had a beerd she says. Why dont you dont have a beerd?

Because I am not God you crazy lady.

I dont say that.

I cant grow a beerd—I am only fifteen.

I dont say that ether.

Can I use your phone? I say.

She lets me in and I start to see how hard this is going to be. I do not know Spencers number. It is in my phone not in my brain. I know the first three numbers because they are the same as mine. But I dont know the others. I stare at the ladys phone and go blank.

Then I remember the cops and phone 911 and they put me on hold. A machine voice tells me what to do. The system is over loded they say. We will reply as soon as we can. Thank you for calling they say. Leave a message they say.

I do not believe it. What if I am being robbed? What if I am on fire?

If you have a medical emergency press 1 says the voice. If you have a police emergency press 2. If you have a—

I want a person I say. The voice doesnt say anything back. I hang up.

I am in a kitchen. The wall paper has flowers on it. The sink is empty. There is a little towel on the frig door. It is a kitchen from a TV ad. If only it was sunny I wuld xpect to see Mr Clean. But it is nite. It is always sunny in Mr Clean ads. He never shows up in nite kitchens.

I try to think what numbers I know apart from 911.

The first one that comes to mind is a pizza place. I do not call that. I think harder and come up with my parents. I phone home and get the machine. It is funny to here my dad telling me to leave my name and number. Dad is so frendly. I take a deep breath and wish I was there insted of here.

I hang up.

Are you ok? asks the old lady. I am in her kitchen dripping with swet and snow and standing a foot taller than her in my skates. She is not scared of me at all. She is staring at me like I am Christmas.

Im trying to remember who I know I say.

You know every body in the world says the old lady. You even know how many hairs they have on there heads.

I dont know what she is talking about. I am thinking of something else. What phone numbers do I know?

Would you like something to read? she says.

I shake my head and think about what other number I know. Police and Pizza and home and who else? Jaden that is who. Jade she is now. My frend from the 15 street possy. I punch the number and there is Jade talking to me.

Hey this is Bunny calling. How are you? I ask.

O yah so it is. Hi Bunny!

Jade is happy like usual when we are talking.

I herd from your brother she says.

You were talking to Spencer?

I am smiling into the phone. If your brother is on the case you feel better. Your brother is on your side.

He came to my work says Jade. He doesnt know where you are. Whats going on?

I got kid napped I say.

What? she says and then says it again. What? Who kid napped you? What do they want? Where are you?

They say they want the anthem. But they are lyers I say. They keep talking about Grampa. I dont know where I am. I dont know whats going on.

And thats for sure.

Poor old Bunny she says.

Jade is rite. I felt ok when I was thinking about Spencer and how he was on the case but not any more. Now talking about all the things I dont know I sound kinda sad and blah. Whats the word for that?

Spencer gave me his phone number she says. You want it?

Yes I say. Thanks.

I tell her to wait a sec and then she reads the number off to me. I rite it on my arm. The old lady has a pen in her desk and I am not taking a chance on forgetting.

Thanks I say again.

Being a hoss stage sucks says Jade. You shuld run away.

I dont have to run I say. I have skates.

She laffs and then asks if I want the possy to come and find me?

Not now I say. The roads are bad for cars. I will have to skate home.

I hang up and call Spencer. The phone rings and rings and someone says that the male box is full and I have to hang up. So I do.

The old lady is watching all this. I go thru it all again. And hang up.

The old lady shakes her head.

Even you cant get thru she says. The phone company is awful.

No one can help. Not Spencer or my parents or Jaden. That is why I feel so pathetic. Thats the word I was trying to think of befor. Sad and blah.

The old lady shows me to the door. I walk careful but my skates are drippy. I say sorry for making a mess of her floor.

She asks where I am going and frowns when I tell her. She has never herd of Creekside. I tell her it is a jail for kids. She nods and says of course.

The poor children there need you she says. There must be so much for you to do.

Well there is Bingo on Friday nites I say.

She tells me the next town is a few miles down the road. She points the way. I thank her. There is a patch of ice in her back yard. I skate across it and hop to the road. I wave back at her.

Grow a beerd she shouts. Then people will know who you are.

THE NEXT TOWN IS RICO.

The sine says it has a pop of 5035. I dont beleeve it. I dont see anyone. There are no lites on and even the McDonalds is closed. In the center of town there is a park area with swings and slides and a guy on a horse. The guy is wearing a three corner hat and a long coat and he is the first person I see.

Hello I say.

Not xpecting an anser because he is made of stone. But he does anser.

Hello he says.

I stop with a jerk and a spray of ice. The guy has not moved. He and his horse are on top of an other bit of stone. He can not really be talking rite?

Hello? I say again. You mean me?

Of course he says.

There are no town lites but the snow is white and the moon is shining enuff for me to see that the three corner hat guy is a statu. The talking is not coming from him.

Where are you? I say.

An old man with a parka and hat comes out from behind some bushes.

We both say hello again.

He tells me about himself. His name is Orvil and he lives next door to the park in the house with the hedge. He is alone. His wife is dead and his son is in Africa and never calls to talk. Orvil was in the back yard when he herd me say hello.

I tell him who I am.

My cousin went to Africa I say.

Does he talk about it?

All the time I say.

Orvils voice is gruff and bumpy—the way a stone can feel in your hand. If the statu culd talk it mite sound like him.

Want to see Jupiter? he says. You shuld see it. Tonite is a good nite. The moons of Gally Layo are clear.

I dont know what he is talking about but he wants to show me so I skate across the snow and ice past the statu to Orvils back yard. In the middle of the yard is something that looks a lot like a machine gun. It is on three legs and it is pointing at the sky. Of course it is not a machine gun. It is a telly scope. When I get close to it Orvil tells me where to put my eyes so I can see Jupiter.

See those moons? he says. Arent they clear?

Wow I say.

But I do not see anything. No Jupiter or stars. No sky. All I see is black. I move my eye back from the eye place and blink. I say Wow again. I am lying because I do not want to hurt Orvils feelings.

Those moons go around Jupiter he says. Gally Layo saw them move 100s of years ago. Witch proved the church was rong.

Thats grate I say.

Orvil says it is not grate at all. The church got mad at Gally Layo and wanted to burn him until he changed his mind and said the moons didnt move after all. And he did and then the church let him live.

Good I say.

But I am rong again. Orvil gets xcited and tells me Gally Layo shuld not have changed his mind. You have to stand up for what you beleeve even if it means dying. Remember that Bunny he says. And nods feercely. Like an eagle or something. Or a dragon. A feerce thing.

Where is the police station in town? I ask.

Theres no police station in town he says. The nearest one is in Perry Vale. Hardly any one lives in Rico in the winter. Me and my son were lonely. And then he went to Africa. And now he doesnt call.

But—I say and then stop talking.

Vi told me about dropping off my note at the police station in town. She was lying. I new Vi was a lyer all ready and this is more proof. No police station. No one to help me. No one to tell my story to. That is why I stop talking.

Orvil goes back to looking at the telly scope. He does not ask me any thing about why I am here or why I am interested in a police station. He is not an asking guy. Or else he knows everything he has to.

I dont.

What day is it? I ask.

Spencer and I went to grampas cottage the day after Christmas—Boxing Day witch is a great name dont you think—how many sports have there own day? I have never herd of soccer day or baseball day or MMA day.

Any way the day after Boxing Day we came back to Toronto and went skating and I got kid napped. And the day after that I escaped and ended up here in Orvils place in Rico. I think thats when things happened. But I dont know.

What day is it today? I ask. Is it new years?

I have to be back at Creekside by new years or I will get in trouble with my prole officer.

Not yet he says looking at his watch. Like it will be new years any minit.

Soon? I ask.

Now he looks up at the sky.

Do you know where Creekside is? I ask. Is it far?

Creekside? he says. New years? he says. You have 2 many questions Bunny. All you need to know is north. And north is that way.

He points at the sky. Like the hole world is a map and he is pointing to the top where the north pole is.

That star will always be there and always show north he says. See the way it is at the end of the handle of the little dipper?

I dont know what he is talking about. The star he is pointing at is small. Is he laffing at me? I cant tell.

I say it was nice to meet him and that maybe his son will call soon.

I will listen for him he says. It is how I herd you.

I glide away. The statu outside his house doesnt say anything.

I head down the road a different way from the way I came. There is no lite exept the moon and it is going behind a thick cloud. The road in front of me is hard to see. I look up. Rite over my head I see a little star that culd be Orvils. It is near a couple of other ones in a bendy line. The clouds are getting thicker now but this little star is shining pretty good.

Turns out its my lucky star. I skate to where the road starts to bend and find exactly what I am looking for. My trip is over.

THE CLOUDS GO LOWER.

Mist swirls around me and blocks what I can see. Thats when I almost run into a metal fence I know—the fence that goes around Creekside. This is perfect. I am not used to looking at it from the outside but the fence is the same. It goes strait up and leans in at the top so you cant clime out.

No body is around. There are lites on but no people. I skate over to the gate and nock but no one comes. Funny eh? They spend a lot of time making it hard to get out of the place but it is not easy to get in ether.

I think how cool it wuld be to break in. They will all be suprised to see me—Greg the gard and Rosco in the kitchen and Mr Wing if he is there and Benj. And Lukas if he is back from Christmas yet. That will be cool all rite.

I skate around the place trying to think of a way in.

Along the back is a ditch I dont remember from last week. It runs beside the fence. It is deep and the ice in it is smooth. I swoosh to the bottom of the ditch and then back up the top fast enough to come off the ground for a second. Witch gives me an idea. Skate borders do this on TV—down and then up the other side. They call it a half pike dont they. Or is that something else. I wonder if I can do it here?

The ditch is on my rite side and the fence is beyond it. No body is around and no body can see any thing because it is so cold and foggy.

I go off for a bit and then turn round and skate back toward the fence. The land is flat and the ice is ok and I am moving fast. When I come to the ditch I woosh down one side and then let myself go coming up the other side. I fly thru the air and land more than half way up the fence. I poke my hand on the barbs and fall down.

Not bad I think. The idea mite work. I try it again only this time I fall over at the bottom of the ditch and make a mess. My breath is coming harder and I am starting to get cold.

Next time is the winner. I bend lower down to go faster and then straiten my legs to jump up as soon I get to the edge of the ditch. The skate borders on TV zoom down one side of the ramp and up the other and they stay in the air for a long time. So do I. I end up near the top of the fence—the leaning part. When your inside Creekside the fence leans the rong way for climing out. But I am climing in. I scramble over and hang on for a second by my mitt. Then the mitt comes off and my hand comes free and I fall into a snow pile.

I am home. My eyes and my pants and shirt and hat and coat are full of snow but I am inside the fence and I am not hurt. Good enuff! I hop forward and find the main bilding. It is starting to snow hard now. I can not see very much. I am shivering and looking forward to bed. There is a key pad where you enter your code to get into the bilding but the lock is frozen. I pull on the door because sometimes it is open any way. And it is. I close it tite.

I am in. The gard room on the left is empty. Greg or who ever is on duty is walking around. My dorm is the middle hall way down the stares. I am staggering with tiredness and reliefness and good to be home ness by now. The lites in the hall are dim and the door to my dorm is open. I xpect Rosco or somebody to wake up and start yelling but he doesnt. I have made it. The surprise will be fun in the morning. I yawn my way out of my coat and skates and pants and shirt and into bed and fall asleep like a lite going out.

RISE AND SHINE!
EVERYBODY UP!

I dont know how many hours it is later but it is not enuff. I pull the covers over my head and go back to sleep. I dont think any one knows I am here. The gard doesnt say anything.

He is new. I hope Greg has not been fired. I like Greg. My first week at Creekside I wuld look thru the fence at the people and dogs who culd move around while I had to stay inside the fence. I didnt do anything—just watched. Some gards yelled at me to get away from the fence and go inside but Greg never did. He new what I was thinking. Once he came over to where I was and we watched a bird floating in the air—a sea gull or something. It sat there on the wind and then swooped away and Greg and I watched it. And he said Yeah and walked away. That was all.

But this gard is not Greg. Ive never herd him befor. He says brekfast is in 15 minits and that means all of us. I hear his footsteps walking away. There are grunts from the other guys.

I am thinking that rite after brekfast I have to call Spencer. I have his number on my arm. He will know who I shuld tell about the kid napping. He is the smart one in the family. I can carry stuff and smile when times are bad—that is what I can do. Spencer knows things. We make a good team.

I peek out from under the covers. 2 strange guys are standing by the door. What are they doing in our dorm? And why are they dressed like this?

Whats with the green suits? I say.

Normally we have orange. I wonder if its green for Christmas or if we are changing colors.

The tall 1 turns around to stare. This is the first thing hes herd me say. He didnt think anyone was in my bed—just covers. I was hoping to surprise everybody. But his surprise is more than I thot.

Whos there? Who said that?

He jumps on me and starts hitting. Why? Jail is tuff but not normally like this. I try and fite back. Its hard because I am under covers and this guy is fast and strong. But I do my best. I grab his hand and say Hey and Woe and like that. And I see real plain and clear that I am in the rong place.

This is not my bedroom. One wall has a big poster with *DO* and *DONT* on it. Another wall has a hole in it. The cover on the lite is broken. These are different from my room. Not much different but a little different. My room has a poster but it says *RULES* not *DO* and *DONT*. And our bathroom is over there insted of over there. And we dont have a hole in our wall. At least we didnt when I left.

So theres that. And then the guys. I am fiting with the big 1 but the little 1 is staring at me like I am a nite mare. A gost or something—witch is funny when I think of what happens later. He puts his hand to his face and screams. Aaaa! he screams and then O my God! and then Aaaa! again. His finger nails are brite red and I see what I shuld have seen befor. The little one is not a guy at all. It is not just the nails. The hair.

The face. The way the suit fits. He is a girl. I mean she. She is a girl.

It is sometimes hard to tell. I have been fooled befor. Mind you I have been fooled by traffic lites befor. I am easy to fool.

As I am getting used to the little guy being a girl I see that the big guy who is punching me in the face and calling me names is also a girl. My face hurts— she is a strong girl. I fall on to the floor and she jumps on me. Just befor she lands on me I twist out of the way. She trys to punch me. I grab her hand and say Sorry.

This isnt my room. I shuld not be here. If someone came to my room I wuld be upset. I mite even fite them. I wonder where I am?

Stop hitting me and I will go find my place I say.

She pulls her hand free and looks me up and down. Her face changes now she is smiling.

Oh no.

She is all dressed and I am not. I took off almost all my close when I got in last nite so I have SpongeBob under pants and a t shirt and that is all. I dive back into bed and pull up the covers.

She—the big one—starts to laff. You beleeve this Teena? she says to the little 1. Who shakes her head.

We shuld TELL on him Teena says. Teena the tiny. She has a little girl voice to go with her name. We shuld get him in TROUBLE she says.

Yeah says the big 1. We can report him rite after he gets dressed. Or maybe befor.

And she laffs some more.

Dont make jokes Bet says Teena.

No please I say. Let me get dressed and I will get out of here and on my way to—

And I stop. I have been so busy fiting that I never thot about my big problem. Now I see it clear. I am not just in the rong room—I am in the rong jail. Creekside does not have girls in it. This is not Creekside.

Oh crap I say. And sink back into bed.

What? says the big 1. Big Bet. She is older than me I think. How did you get here? she asks. What is going on?

I shake my head.

Come on! she says but I cant tell her.

Her nose is bent side ways and when she frowns it bends even more. Whatever is going on it is messed she says.

Yah I say.

Whatre we gonna DO? asks the other one. Teena. She is still standing by the door. She is older than me 2 but she sounds little and winy. We shuld TELL on him she says.

Hes in enuff trouble says Bet.

He slept in our ROOM says Teena. Hes a boy and he was HERE. He mite have seen us getting DRESSED!

She has her hand to her mouth again. The nails are like straw berrys. How culd I ever think she was a boy?

He was sleeping so he didnt see anything says Bet. And what does it matter if he saw our under wear? We saw his SpongeBobs huh? Besides if we tell on him who is going to get in trouble? We are—that is who. Remember when Marthas boy frend stayed after visitors hours? Thats what will happen to us.

But its not FAIR! says Teena. What do we DO?

We get him out of here says Bet.

They look at each other. They both want me to go away but they are not on the same side. Bet wants to do something and Teena doesnt.

Well I am HUNGRY says Teena.

Go on to brekfast then says Bet. I will take care of him.

Does she mean it?

Can I drink your chocolate milk? says Teena.

No says Bet.

Teena scrunches up her face and stomps out the door.

OK SAYS BET.

I will help you. But first what is your name?

I shake my head. I dont want to tell her. I dont want to give her anything.

OK she says again. Get dressed. I wont look.

She turns away and I pull on my close. The air is warm and smells like cement and soap. Better than Creekside.

I want to make sure.

How do I know you will help me get out? I ask her.

Cause I said I wuld.

But why shuld I beleeve you?

She doesnt turn around. I can see her sholders bunch up under her suit.

Are you calling me a lyer? she says.

Maybe I say.

I am thinking about Vi. I beleeved her and I was rong.

Bet doesnt talk for a second. The hole in the wall is about the size of a fist. And it is about the same place her fist wuld be if she punched the wall.

Are you dressed yet? she says. Can I turn round?

Yes I say.

So she turns and she is mad all rite. Her face was dark befor but it is darker now. Her eyes are thin and her hands are fists.

I am a bad girl she says. The judge said so. I do not have a lot going for me. I am not rich or pretty and my parents dont love me. I am a JO—I broke my uncles arm and I am here because of it she says. I am angry a lot of the time. But I do what I say I will do. My frend Tracy lives in my bilding back home she says. Tracy isnt my mom or anything but she gives good advice. Keep your word she says. If you say you are going to do something do it. No matter how it turns out you will be able to live with yourself because you did what you said you would do. Your word is good.

Bet is looking away from me. She is thinking about her frend Tracy. Her eyes are long distance. She is knowing things. Vi never looked like that. Not even when she kissed me.

I said I wuld help you says Bet. And I will. Or I will go down trying to help you. If you dont trust me— well you wont. But you will be rong.

A bell rings some where down the hall and the lites go off in the dorms. They do this in Creekside to save energy. We are supposed to go to the common areas now—gym or dining hall or class.

Bet doesnt move. The whites of her eyes disappear and then come back when she blinks. I cant say when someone is lying but sometimes I can tell when they are not. Bet is not.

My name is Bunny I say.

She nods. I put out my hand and we shake. Her hands are as big as mine.

My hall looks just like this I say. Thats why I broke in last nite. Sorry. Now I have to get back to Creekside befor my Christmas pass runs out. Thanks for helping I say.

She looks away.

Whats a JO? I ask.

Juvenile offender she says.

Oh.

And why did you break your uncles arm? I ask.

None of your dam business.

THE ONLY REASON
I HAVENT BEEN FOUND
OUT YET

is cause of the holidays. Other girls normally live in this room along with Teena and Bet. I was in 1 of there beds last nite.

And we dont have much time says Bet. Teena is a chatty girl. She will talk even tho she shuldnt. Skrillex will find out.

Skrillex is a gard? I say.

She is awful. She makes you want to scream. Come with me now.

I start toward the door.

Stop says Bet. Walk slower and swing your hips.

She found a green jump suit that is almost my size and I have it on and also a big towel around my head.

Hows this? I ask.

Pretty bad says Bet. You make an ugly girl Bunny.

She is smiling but not with her eyes. She carries a green garbage bag. I am wearing sandals that hide my guy feet and are better to walk in than my skates witch are in the garbage bag along with my coat and hat.

The hall is brite like at Creekside. Lots of ways the 2 places are the same. The noise bounces around off the same hard walls and floors. The windows have the same bars on them.

A couple of guys go past talking about home. Sorry girls not guys. But they are talking the same as if this was Creekside and they were guys. One of them says how her home sucks and the other one says yah but it is better than here. Then they are past.

Take your hands out of your pockets Bunny says Bet. You just washed your hair. Thats why you have the towel. Use it to hide your hands.

Rite.

Visiting is in the caf like at Creekside. Bets plan is sneek me in so I can go out later with the other visitors.

It is a good plan. All I need is a place to change back into a boy. And a reason to be there.

Who am I visiting? I ask.

Me you dummy says Bet. You can be my—

And she stops.

I know what she is thinking. Who can I be? Brother isnt rite. I am a lot whiter than her. Cousin maybe. But probly not.

Frend I say. I can be your frend visiting from Toronto or someplace.

Where? she says.

Toronto. You know—where the Maple Leafs are from.

I heard of it she says. Making a joke.

Some other girls are coming toward us. I dont see them—just there jump suits. I hide my head in the towel. I am afraid of bumping into a wall so I slow down.

I hear them say Hey Bet. I smell something sweet. Candy or something.

Hey says Bet.

I have to act like a girl but all I am doing is standing. Do girls stand different from guys? I never noticed.

Whos this? says a new voice. Shes a big one isnt she?

This heres Bunny says Bet. She just got here. Shes in C dorm with me.

Hi Bunny says a few voices. I hear them like a waterfall. Hi Hi Hi. I nod my towel.

Bunny cant talk on account of her cold says Bet. It came on sudden after she washed her hair. Her voice drys up. Rite Bunny?

I nod.

Bunnys mom is coming to visit today so Im taking her to the visitors room says Bet.

I feel a hand on my elbow and hear her saying This way. A minit later I smell soap and cleaner and bathroom tile. I know where we are. I listen for voices and sounds of splashing or flushing but there arent any—we are alone.

Can I take off my towel? I ask.

Shh says Bet. Wernt supposed to be here.

She pushes me into a what do you call it—a place with a toilet—and throws the bag in after me. A stall. Thats what I mean.

Get changed quick and I will take you in to the visitors room she says.

I put on my old shirt and pants so I am a boy again. Its hot.

I hear a new voice outside. Not Bets. A woman it sounds like.

Hell she says.

Bets towel is on the toilet seat. I put it back on—in case.

Hell says the new voice. Hell hell hello Bet. Watcha watcha watcha doin here?

Her breath comes in pants in between her talking. Watcha pant pant watcha doin?

Skrillex says Bet.

Yournot she says. Yournot allowed yournot yournot yournot allowed—

Allowed in here on visitors day? Bet cuts in. Your rite Skrillex.

Skrillex is the gard who drives Bet crazy. If she talks like this all the time I beleeve it.

I was on my way to brekfast and I just had to go says Bet. Sorry.

Sorry? says Skrillex. Not so so so so so so so sorry enuff. This is out of bounds. Out of out of bounds. Im counting she says. Im counting the strokes youll get for breaking bounds. Can you gess? Gess how many? How many strokes? Can you can you can you?

I hear Bet thru the door of the stall. She goes Huhhh. Its always 14 she says.

Thats rite says Skrillex. Im counting to counting to 14. Im counting til counting til your sorry for breaking the rules. You are in so much so much so so so so so so much—

Trouble says Bet. I know.

Do you know what Im holding? Do you? Do you? Do you? Do you? Do you? Do you? Do you? Do you? Do you? Do you? Do you? Do you? Thats 13 times I said it. Dont move girl. Do you? There thats 14. Thats when I can start to start to when I can start to—

She breaks off. I hear a smacking sound like a punch or a kick.

Ow! says Bet.

There says Skrillex. Thatll teach you. Thatll—thatll—thatll—thatll—thatll—

With every *thatll* theres an other smacking sound. Skrillex is hitting Bet.

I cant let her take my punishment because of me. I dont think what I am doing. I throw open the door of my stall. Theres 2 people in the room—Bet and an old lady with a cane witch she is holding like a club. Bet is rubbing her leg where the lady must of hit her with the cane. The lady stares up at me with her evil old eyes.

Skrillex.

She is tiny like an elf. I am 2wice as big as she is. The cane is a thin bit of wood like a marsh mallow tosting stick. Every thing about her is little xept for her long long long long—now I am sounding like her— hair. And her eyes. They are huge and round and full of fire. She stares at me like—I dont know—like the sun. I think of her hitting Bet and I am mad. Bet is big and Skrillex is little and her cane probly doesnt hurt much but I am still mad. I think of the judge telling Bet she is no good. That makes me mad 2.

Skrillex gasps. What? she says to me. What what what what are you?

What does she think I am? Over her sholder is a meer and I see myself in it. I look stupid with the big white towel on my head but Skrillex isnt looking at my towel. Its so hot I have my sleeve rolled up and shes staring at the tattoo on my arm. She takes a step back.

Fiff she says. Then again. Fiff. Fiff fiff fiff—

I think fast. Well I cant—but I think as fast as I can.

15 I say.

Thats what she is trying to say. My tatoo is a 15 with a candle. I sort of belong to a street gang called the 15 Street Possy. Sort of. Its a long story.

NO! yells Skrillex. 14 14 14 14 14 is a good number. Not that not not—

15 I say again.

Bet is looking hard and thinking hard.

Its always 14 with you she says. You do things 14 times. Ive seen you counting. You walk 14 steps and then turn left. We all wonder. Why not keep going? 10 11 12 13—

14! Skrillex wispers in a voice that kind of creeps me out. 14! she wispers again.

Im holding the bag with skates in it. When the skate blades hit each other it sounds like chains. With my towel on and my chains does Skrillex think I am somebody else? A gost? Maybe she does. She is not like the sun now. Her eyes are scared.

Daddy! says Skrillex still in her creepy wisper. Why Daddy why? Daddy likes 14. Daddy likes Daddy likes 14. But not fiff not fiff not fiff not not not—

She points at my arm.

Why Daddy? she asks.

I take a step out of the stall. Skrillex looks back at the door like she wants to run. But she is not a scaredy cat. She swings her cane at me.

I catch it in my free hand. It stings but I dont care. I am thinking of all the girls Skrillex has hit with the cane. I pull the cane out of her hand. Now I am holding it.

I drop my bag witch makes the skates clash. I swing Skrillex cane hard and hit the side of the stall. A thin sharp whippy sound bounces around the room. I do it again. And again. And again. And again and again and again and again. Bets head moves up and down.

Thats 12 she says. Shes been counting. I hit the stall again.

Skrillex starts to shake. Got she says. Pant. Got got got got gotta go.

The cane breaks but I keep on hitting with the bit in my hand. Bet counts along with my hits. Smash. 13. Smash 14. Skrillex is shaking like a broken machine. Arms out wide and hair in her eyes. Things fall out of her pockets.

15!

Bet holds the bathroom door open and Skrillex runs. Turns out she doesnt need her cane.

IT IS A BIT LATER

—maybe an hour maybe a bit longer. A lot has happened. I am full of pancakes and juice. I am skating away from Bet and Skrillex and Teena and the rest of them. The sun is shining and my shadow is bouncing around on the road and the ground in front of me.

I talked to my brother. Finally. Skrillex dropped her phone along with everything else and Bet handed it to me and I phoned the number on my arm. It was great to hear his voice.

Bunny? he said. And then he said my name again. Bunny! Oh my god, you remembered my number. Where are you? Are you all rite?

It was nice to hear how worryed Spencer was. That doesnt sound rite but you know what I mean.

Jade gave me your number I said. I called her.

You've been gone 2 days now Bun. Are you okay? Can you talk? asked Spencer. Witch was silly because thats what we were doing.

I'm pretty hungry I said.

Bet herd me say this and grabbed my arm. She led me down a dark cement hall with 2 doors at the end. There was a sine painted over 1 of the doors. *Visitors Only* it said. She pushed me thru it into a big room with windows and sunshine and people eating. I blinked. This was way nicer than our caf at Creekside. Xept for the gards.

Spencer asked where I was so he culd come and get me witch sounded great. But I didnt know where I was yet. There was a big map on the wall but I didnt see it until later.

I wonder what wuld happen—what it wuld of been like—if I saw the map and told Spencer where I really was? He wuld of beleeved me but then what—wuld he still say he culd come and get me? Anyway I didnt see the map yet. I started by telling Spencer about the house I skated away from. The Newman place.

They put me in the basement I said but I culd see things out the window.

What can you see now? he asked.

Now?

Yes rite now.

I wasnt at the Newman place now but Spencer is smarter than me and he wanted to know so I went over to the window and looked out.

I can see a fence and a road I told him. And some stores in the distance. And a guy talking on the phone like us. And a speed limit sine by the road. It says 30.

He wanted to know more so I told him there was a muffler place and a pizza place. He wanted to know what kind.

I told him it had the blu sine with the white holes.

Dominos! he shouted.

The name of the pizza place. He asked if there was a Christmas reath in the window but I culdnt see because it was far away. I told him I culd see a wall and an alley.

And the wall is covered with tags like the gym on 15 Street! he shouted. Witch it was. I never thot of that I said.

By the way did you know that gym and jim are not the same? I was amazed when Mr Wing told me. Jim is the guys name and gym is the place. So Jim can go to the gym—I think thats it. Doug and dug are different 2. And brian and brain. But not Rob and rob—they are the same. You can rob Rob on your way home from the gym.

On my report card Mr Wing said my spelling still needs work.

Spencer wanted to know my street number but I didnt know. And wuld you really need the number anyway? Its a jail. Wuldnt you just tell the pizza guy to deliver to the place with the big fence and the armed gards?

Visitors day here was a lot like at Creekside. The caf was full of jail girls and there moms and dads and frends. You culd tell the jail girls because they were in green suits. It wasnt very noisy. People are quiet when they are sad and when they are eating.

My phone—Skrillex phone—beeped. I held it away from my ear. 3% power it said.

Spencer told me they were on their way and to be careful. I gess he new how slippery it was outside.

I wanted to know more about why they kid napped me. He said it went back to Grampa being a spy and that it was Grampa in the movy. Hed been talking to somebody named Susan. I asked about her and he said not Susan—Dusan.

Its a guy he said. He has a beerd.

Dusan—ok.

I didnt know if Grampa was a good guy or not. But Vi and Lubor and maybe this Dusan with the beerd were the kid nappers. That made them the bad guys. And me and Spencer were working against them.

He told me that made us the good guys and that they were on there way and to stay cool. I said I wuld and he hung up.

My brother. A guy who was on my side all the time. Everybody shuld have 1 of those.

I filled a plate with pancakes and found Bet and had brekfast with her. She told me to eat fast and then go. That because I was a guy I culd walk out the main door and be free.

I said thank you again and she said forget it and I said I never wuld.

You said youd help me and you did I said.

We talked about Skrillex and how weird she was.

What was that about her dad? I asked.

Shes old—I never thot of her having a dad said Bet. Maybe he did something when she was 15. Maybe he left. My dad left when I was little.

I said I was sorry. Bet shrugged. It was a long time ago she said.

We chewed our pancakes. Teena frowned from a few tables over and then looked away. Pretending I wasnt there. OK with me.

Anyway its lucky Skrillex saw your tatoo Bet said. Now I know shes scared of 15 and when shes being mean I can start counting and freak her out. Thanks Bunny.

And then I saw the map on the wall. I went over and stared at it but it didnt make sense. Bet came over and pointed stuff out. I said no way. She xplained. The words were there on the paper all rite. I new where I was. O crap.

I took out the Skrillex phone. Spencer wuld tell me what to do. But the call didnt work. Bet took the phone and said it was out of power. Thats what the 3% ment.

Spencer culdnt come to get me. It was up to me to get home.

I told Bet I had to leave rite then. And I did. We shook hands at the door and the gards let me out. Bet waved.

And now it is an hour later. Maybe a bit longer.

I AM SKATING DOWN
THE STREET

with my shadow ahead of me. I know a hole lot that I didnt know befor. Bets jail is called the Joy center for youth rehab. Really—Joy. Somebody has a great sense of humor. It has the same bildings and the same fence as Creekside witch is why I thot I was home when I saw it. I sort of know where Joy is—where I am I mean. I have to keep the sun behind me if I am going to get home witch will take longer than I thot. I will not get there tonite.

Even tho Spencer cant help me Im feeling pretty good. I didnt want to trust Bet but I did and that worked out ok. Skrillex will probly not hit her again.

I still dont know why Bet broke her uncles arm.

I come to the edge of town. There is a rink and a couple of kids are playing hockey with an old man. There skates look new.

I get a sudden strong memory of shopping for skates with Grampa. I was maybe in grade 5 and there was a spotted puppy scratching its ears on the floor. Grampa asked for the best pair in the store.

Try these Bernard he said. He always called me Bernard witch is my long name. Every one else calls me Bunny because that is frendlier and more like me. I only hear the name Bernard in Grampa's voice. Your problem is Bernard. What you need Bernard. You shuld be doing this thing Bernard.

We were shopping for skates because he wanted me to play hockey.

Your a good skater Bernard he said. A big tuff boy like you shuld be going into the corners. You arent afraid of corners are you?

I didnt know what he ment. Why would I be afraid of corners? I asked.

Good for you he said.

Sometimes I dont know where to go I said. A corner means you can go different ways. Choice is tricky I said. But not scary.

We brought the skates home and Grampa told Mom about me playing hockey.

Do you want to play hockey? she asked me.

Sure he does said Grampa. Hockey is a tuff guy sport and Bunny is a tuff guy.

Am I? I said.

What do you think we were talking about back there at the store? he said.

I dont know I said.

I never know what we are talking about. I was looking at the puppy I said.

You shuld listen harder Bernard he said.

Grampa wanted me to do better all the time. What does that mean? If a guy wants you to do better he must think you are not doing very well.

I wonder what he wuld say to me now. A hoss stage who escaped and broke into a girls jail and escaped again. Who is on his way home without food or money or a phone. And home is a long way— longer than I thot.

Grampa is dead so of course he wuldnt really say much now. Only whatever you say when you are under ground—its dark in here I gess he wuld say.

But if he was alive and standing beside me what wuld he say? Probly he wuld say Do better.

Maybe he is rite. But I am doing my best. I dont think I can do any better than that.

The family on the rink are practicing. Grampa is teaching the boy and girl how to pass. Shoot it at me KC he says. Aim a little ahead. And soft KC. Soft! Or I will miss he says. KC is the girl. She fires the puck way ahead of Grampa and way hard.

You missed she says.

He gets the puck and passes to the boy. Pass it back he says.

They talk like the old lady who thot I was God. The guy with the telly scope sounded the same. Like me but not quite like me. Now I know why.

I hop over the bords and head down the rink. There's an exit at the far end—a hole in the bords. I head for that. The ice is smooth and clean. Better than the road.

The family watch me. Hey mister you skate good says the little girl KC.

I am not used to being called Mister. I spin round so I am facing her and keep going backward.

Showing off a little. Thanks I say.

Do you wanna stay and play with us? she asks. Grampa can he play with us?

Yah says the boy. Hes good.

Yah hes good all rite. Dyou wanna play son? he says to me.

They are all having fun together. I shake my head. Got to get home I say.

Are you crying? asks the girl.

No I say. I am thru the bords now.

Why is he crying Grampa? she asks.

I am gone.

I AM IN THE MIDDLE OF THE COUNTRY SIDE

heading toward the river witch I know I have to cross. Roads are narrow and icy xept when they are wide and icy. I pass car after car after stopped car. And truck. Some are in the ditch. Some are busted. None of them can go. I gess in the city everything is salted and sanded but out here it is a day for no cars.

I am feeling ok. Really. I miss Spencer. I miss mom and dad. I miss Jade even tho we havent seen each other in a while. I sort of miss my cousins. DJ is always sure what to do. Whether it is rite or not he is always sure. I culd use some of that now. I wonder if DJ will get in trubble now? Trouble I mean.

He was sort of looking after me and I got kid napped. It wuld be 2 bad if he got in trouble—it is not his falt.

My cousin Adam is from New York. Spencer stayed over at his place when he was on his way to kiss that actress. Huh. I shuld of looked harder at the map in the Joy jail. Maybe I wuld of seen Adams place.

Swoosh swish. My shadow is to the rite of me and way out in front. It is like I am a huge snake or a train or something. That is what my shadow looks like.

You know what I do not miss—jail. Creekside or Joy ether. Being locked up is not fun. Flying down the road like this is the opposite of being in jail. Dad sings a song about a river you can skate away on. It is a pretty cool song. If I new the words I wuld sing it now. I dont know them but I know the tune. I hum a bit.

I keep my rite hand in my pocket. It is the one without a glove. I lost it on the fence at the Joy jail and now I dont have it. My hand is okay in my pocket. Things culd be worse. Some people have no shoes. If I had no shoes I culd not put my feet in my pockets.

I hear loud noises of scraping and grinding from behind me. I move to the side of the road as here comes a tow truck—the kind with a long flat bed.

Sitting on top of the truck is a little car with a camera sticking out of the top. The front of the car is smashed. The sine on the side says *GOOGLE*. The camera is still working. It turns to point at me as it goes past. I wave. I am going to be on google maps if anyone wants to get here.

I have to pee. That is easy because I am alone. Nothing but fields all around me. Its a good thing I was not peeing when the google car went by.

Things do get worse now. My left skate is undone and when I bend over to tie it again the lace breaks. *Bang*. Or more like *Thwap*. I end up lying in the road holding a piece of lace. This is not a big bad thing like being kid napped or being cold and late and a long way from home. Witch is also true for me. But it seems really really bad. I was not upset befor but I am now. I am healthy and free and I dont have to pee any more but I almost start crying over a skate lace. Funny eh?

And then I hear Santa.

Jingle Jingle Jingle.

Dammit Rudolf!

Jingle.

Stop Rudolf! Stop! I say. Dammit stop!!

Thats what I hear. Its not really him but Santa is what I think when I hear the jingling and the name. And this is a good place to see Santa—a real old fashioned winter picture with snow and ice and some forest and a lot of quiet. I used to think of him flying down from the North Pole every year on just this kind of evening.

A horse is pulling a sled toward me. Perfect for the seen. It has those big runner things that bend up in the front. Bells hang on the what are they—the rains. The driver pulls on them and the sled finally stops.

Want some help? he calls to me.

I am trying to figure him out. Hes fat and he has a beerd and he drives a sled with jingle bells—but he has a horse insted of rain deer and his sled doesnt fly and his beerd and coat are brown. Hes like Santas poor little brother.

I think about that for a sec—life at home with a big brother who brings home A+ report cards and gives presents to the poor. His parents and teachers go on about how wonderful he is. That Nickolas is a saint! And mean while this guy is not doing so well. Every body is shaking there heads saying he wont amount to anything. A saint—dont joke with me.

Hmm. These thots are getting close to my home life. Spencers teachers like him and mine dont think much of me. The only A I ever got was at Creekside this year. Mr Wing liked the story I rote about getting that 15 tatoo.

When I get back I will rite up this hoss stage and skating story. I wonder how it will end? I hope Mr Wing likes it.

All this time the driver stares down at me. You wanna lift there pal? he says. Lemme help you out.

I need help so I hop over to his sled and climb on and soon enuff we are swooshing down the road with the horse Rudolf clopping ahead. I am trying to fix my skate lace—taking it out and tying a not and putting it back in. It isnt working.

While we drive the guy tells me all about himself. His name is Steve. I ask if he has a brother named Nickolas and he says no. He has no brothers or sisters or mom and dad. He is 24 years old and lives in a house in the next town witch is where he is going now.

Are you close to the river? I ask.

The saint low rents?

Thats it!

I dont know the way it is spelled but thats what Bet said when I asked about it. Low rents. I told myself to remember that name and then I forgot.

Its not far from my house says Steve.

Great I say and go back to fixing my skate. Witch is not going great. The lace keeps breaking. I have 3 nots now and my lace is getting shorter and shorter.

You look like you mite need a new lace pal says Steve.

He calls me pal. That is okay.

We can get you some in town he says. The store shuld be open. I have to stop there anyway. Its not far he says.

Thanks I say.

I check my pockets for money. I had 5 dollars when I went skating. Spencer was going to buy me a hot dog but I was kid napped befor he got back so I never payed him.

The money is in my back pocket. Good.

My hand is warm now. It was getting cold after all the time I spent trying to make nots in the lace. I keep it in my pocket and lean over.

You ok pal? asks Steve.

Sure I say.

We are sledding over a field of snow. The road is beside us on the left side. There are woods on the rite. We are coming to a traffic lite—the first in a while. Steve pulls on the rains and tells the horse to slow down. He pulls harder. He yells. We bump off the field and onto the road and past the traffic lite.

Dammit Rudolf! yells Steve. Why dont you do what I want? You mite as well be my kid!

I laff. Mom yells at me all the time for not doing what she wants.

Steves town is called Perivale. We pass the sine. Theres houses and stores and street lites and a big Christmas tree in front of the town hall. And a school and an other one and a donut shop and a Burger King and 2 stop lites. And some pick up trucks driving slowly. Steve tells me that Perivale is the biggest town in the county. He says there are even more people there on Saturdays when the farmers come in for the market.

The store is called Food Land. It is down the main street from the town hall. We stop. Steve fastens

Rudolf to one of the lite posts. We are the only sled in the parking lot.

Gess what? They sell skate laces. And other things that you dont normally see at a food store—fire wood and nails and socks and glasses and folding chairs and beer. Huh. There are people putting all these things in shopping carts.

The laces cost $3.95 but befor I can pay Steve takes out his wallet. He is standing behind me in the line holding a big bag of food for Rudolf. Oats I gess.

All together he says to the checkout lady.

Are you sure? I ask him.

I like to help people he says.

He hands me the laces—and also a mitt.

I saw you are missing a glove he says. Take it. Its a mitt—it can be left or rite he says.

Where did you get it? I say.

I lost the other 1 says Steve. So you shuld have it.

It is brown with wooly stuff sticking out. It is pretty heavy.

Well thanks I say. Thanks Steve.

I hop over to the Food Land door and sit down so I can do up my other skate. Only I cant do it.

The laces are in a plastic pack and I cant get it open no matter how hard I try.

Dont you hate that? Who decides to make a pack so tite nobody can get in it? Who ever he is I wish he was here so I could make him break his fingers and teeth trying to get the laces. Id still be there going crazy xept that Steve hands me a sort of nife. You push the blade in and out with your thum. I nife open the pack and in 5 minits I am ready to go. The other lace is in my pocket.

Thanks Steve I say. Thanks a lot.

He tells me to keep the nife for now. You mite need it agane he says.

We go out of the store together. It is dark now— winter dark witch means afternoon snack time. Summer dark is bed time. Steve asks do I want anything else?

Like what? I say.

I dunno he says. Anything.

I dont have to think very hard.

Do you have a phone? I ask.

He smiles. You can call from my place he says. Lets go there now.

Rudolf makes a horse noise. He smells the oats.

STEVES PLACE IS TALL AND POINTY

and takes up a lot of the block. It looks like a fort or a castle xept for the front porch. Not many castles have a porch. An old lady lets us in. This is Onny says Steve. She looks after the house for me. Maybe he means Annie but he says it like Onny and that is what I call her when I say hi. She doesnt call me anything just ducks her head and smiles. Steve asks Onny if her son has come yet. She shakes her head. Steve tells me that Onnys son and his wife live close by and come over every week for dinner. Youll meet them later Steve says to me.

I didnt know I was staying for dinner. But I am hungry. Sure I say.

We are in a white and black and red hall with a closet big enough for all the close I ever wore and a ceiling tall enough to be the ceiling on the second floor. Near the closet is a guy in armor. A nite. I say hi because he looks like a person and then I blush. I know hes not real. Im not surprised when he doesnt say anything back.

Steve asks Onny to take me to a spare bedroom. She ducks her head again and shows me up a lot of stares and down a few halls to a room with everything in it—bed and desk and lamp and bookcase and computer and bath tub and sink and TV and meer. And phone. All rite maybe not everything but a lot. There is a picture of a girl and an other picture of a tiger in a forest. The girl is wearing faraway close and has a jug sitting on her head. The tiger is hidden in the grass. All I can see are the stripes and the eyes.

There is a cooky jar. Onny opens it for me. Oatmeal—nice. Everybody likes them. I ask if she wants a cooky but she is gone. Her footsteps get softer as she walks away.

I think about lying down on the bed but I mite sleep forever. I dont want to do that. I want to talk to Spencer. The phone is an old time one with places to put your finger and turn. I check my arm for Spencers number and dial it. He doesnt answer. His message comes on. To leave a message I have to press 9 but there is no way to press a number on this phone.

I have to go to the bathroom. It is real comfortable in there. The seat is warm as soon as I sit down—like it is heated. One of the books on the shelf beside me is called A Local Hero and it is about Steve. His picture is on the cover. I have never seen a book about anyone I know and here I am in his house. On his toilet. I open the book and read about stuff Steve does to help people. I dont know how long I keep reading but it is after I am finished on the toilet.

I go down some stares and wander around. It takes me a while to find people. I smell smoke from a fireplace and hear voices befor I get to the room with the talking. Steve says the roads are real bad tonite. If they are still bad next week call me or Onny he says. I can come out with Rudolf and give you a lift.

I gess the son and his wife are here. I am all set to go in and meet them—and then Steve says a name that freezes me.

Who is Dusan? he says.

I stop walking. They are in the room at the end of the hall. The door is open and I can see the flicker on the wall that comes from the fire lite.

I thot you said Susan at first but Dusan is a guys name. Who is he? says Steve.

He is the head of our sell says a new voice. A guy. Dusan is our boss says this guy.

He is disappointed in us rite now says another new voice—a woman. Somebody is missing and Dusan blames us she says.

The voices make my hands clench up into fists and my hart starts to zoom around like a race car. I know the woman and the man.

Thats 2 bad says Steve. Can I help?

Dusan is the name Spencer told me about—the guy who called him about Grampa. I wuld of walked into the room if I had not talked to Spencer. But the name Dusan made me stop and now Ive herd Lubor and Vi and I know that the room is dangerous.

I am the missing person they are talking about. They want me.

I sneek back the way I came. There is soft carpeting and my feet sink into it. I run into Onny. She is holding a tray with things on it. Drinks and things. She nods at me and makes a move with her tray like she is shooing me along the hall to the living room.

I dont want to speak because Lubor and Vi mite hear. I hold up my hands to Onny to say wait. I point upstares. Then I spread my fingers to say 10. I shake them at Onny so she knows I will be back down in 10 minits. I hear Steves voice again.

I wonder where Bunny is? he says.

Bunny? says Lubor. Who is Bunny?

Lubor all rite—he says Bunnee.

Bunny is a new frend of mine says Steve. I ran into him this afternoon on the road. He is an interesting young man.

He? says Vi. A guy named Bunny?

Oh crap I think.

Lubors voice is louder.

Mama!

I turn. He shouts from the door way down the hall. At least I gess it is him. Ive never seen him without his red mask. Hes as big as I remember. His face is dark—not like Bets or Jades but dark for a white guy. Like Onnys I gess. His hair grows in a point on his for head.

Mama! he shouts. Stop that boy!

Onny moves to block me and her tray tips. The drinks slide. She doesnt want mess in Steves house. She saves the tray and I get past her to the stares. Voices bubble up behind me. Lubors and Steves and Vis. She points at me. Her face is moving around.

You she says. Just—you. But the way she says it is like an arrow aiming rite at me. Why did I think she was nice? Why did I trust her?

I have to get out of here. I head down stares.

THE NEXT BIT IS CRAZY.

I run around the house and they all run after me. Its scary like a dream is scary and it stretches out like a dream 2. Sometimes it seems like time is stopping. I get lost rite away. There is a hall in front of me and I take the first turn to the left and then there is an other hall and I take an other turn and there is still more hall in front of me. The house is like a what do you call it—a maze. The halls all have white walls and doors and pictures and shelfs and lites so they look the same. A few times I think I am in a hall I have been in befor xept the shelfs have different things on them. Books and candles and pots and like that. Steve has a lot of things and I gess he has to put them somewhere. Sometimes there are a few stares going down to a little door. Or they go up and there is an other hall. Or they go down and then up again for no reason at all. I keep running. If there was a camera showing the hole house it mite look like Scooby Doo. Me running here and them running there. Now and then I hear a bang or a voice but mostly it is quiet. We all keep on missing each other.

Even tho I think about Scooby I dont laff.

I come to some stares but do not take them because this time I see an other way to go—a rite turn. I take it and come to a hall with a picture of trees and a wooden box and a left turn and now all at once the floor is different. I stop. This is the red and white and black room with the closet and the nite in armor and the tall ceiling. This is where I came in.

My coat is on the back of a chair. I put it on. My skates are side by side on the floor. The 13 from the city hall rental place is on the back. I sit to lace them on.

Steve steps out from behind the closet and hands me a bag.

I am sorry you are going to miss dinner he says. Here are sandwiches for your journey.

I put them in my coat pocket. Steve holds the front door open for me.

I dont know what to say to him.

Im not—

I dont finish.

Vi and Lubor are—

I dont finish that ether.

Who are you? I say finally.

He doesnt answer my question. Main street is that way he says. Down the road and across the vacant lot. Turn rite and keep going. In a few miles you will see sines for the bridge.

No who are you really? You got my stuff ready for me I say. You gave me sandwiches. Your helping me. Does that mean you are on my side?

I try to give every body what they want he says.

Every body?

As many as I can.

But—every body? I say. Even bad guys?

He blinks. Who are they? he says.

Forget it I say.

He is still holding the door open. Go fast he says.

I hop out the door and down the steps. Steve shuts the door. My skates cut into the ice on the front walk.

Theres a long drive way on my rite with a black car parked behind the sled. I give a little shudder—I know that car. I was in the trunk.

I get an idea.

In my pocket I find the nife that Steve gave me to open the plastic pack. You mite need that sometime he said. I skate over to the car.

Lite shines out at me. The door is open agane and I hear Steves voice.

There he is! he says. There in the drive way!

He means me. He is telling Lubor and Vi where I am. He is helping them.

Wow! He really is on every bodys side.

I stab the back tire of the car—the nearest tire. It has a chain on it so it can go on icy roads. My nife bounces off the chain. Lubor and Vi run down the walk waving there arms and shouting. I stab again and this time the nife goes into rubber and I hear the whoosh of air coming out. The car sinks slow and steddy like gramma sitting down in the living room. Lubor falls but not like gramma—this is like going off the diving board and landing on your back. *Wump*. His legs wave in the air like a bug. Like a bugs legs. He says something in his axent voice.

Here comes Vi. I dont think of her kissing me or telling me she was on my side. I am not done with the car yet. I skate round to the other back tire.

Bunny! Stop!

Vi is at the end of the drive in her sweater. If I think of her lying to me I will get mad. I stick my nife into the other back tire and the air whooshes and I do not think of Vi. Now the car cant go. There is a spare tire in the trunk—I remember. But there arent 2 spare tires.

I kick it—Vi's car. Full of her stuff. I do not think of her kissing me. Why did I trust her? The air is clear and cold and still. Vi moves toward me with slidey steps but she will not catch me tonite. I turn and dash away. My skates feel good and tite on my feet. The road is covered in ice. No one will be able to catch me for a while.

I dont know how you can give every body what they want. What if 2 people want to win the same race? Some body has to lose. Just now I wanted to get away and Lubor and Vi wanted to catch me and Steve wanted to help us both. Thats weird—isnt it?

The street lites bounce and sparkle. The road goes strait and ends at a vacant lot the way Steve says it will.

A guy is standing in the middle of the vacant lot with a hose in his hand. There is a rink there and he is flooding it to make it smooth. He sees me and turns off the hose.

Cmon kiddo he yells. The ice is fine.

I dash across. The ice is already hard and really smooth. Theres a big road on the other side of the vacant lot. I remember what Steve said.

Does this road go to the bridge? I ask.

Thats the 37 he says.

Does it go to the bridge to Canada?

Course he says.

He makes it seem like I am stupid for not knowing this. Everybody knows the 37 goes to Canada. I thank him and start away.

Why dyou want to go to Canada kiddo? he calls after me. Its full of Canadians.

I cant tell if he is laffing. It mite be a joke and it mite not. I mean he is rite—Canada is full of Canadians. I keep skating and dont say anything.

I was in the USA for a long time without knowing it. I really did think I was in Canada until I saw the map at the jail. I can see why. The big things are not different. The trees and snow and clouds are the same. And the roads and cars and stores and people are the same. Little things are different—licence plates and speed limits and the way they say roof. That is funny. Roof. It sounds like ruff. And about sounds like abat. They all talk like that—Steve and the old lady and Orvil and the kids skating with there grampa. But really the places are more the same than they are different. The same moon is in the sky. So is the little star pointing me north—but I cant find it now but Im sure its there.

I am alone on the road. After a few alone minits I see a sine—*Bridge to Canada 2 miles*. I eat a sandwich from my pocket. I have to take off my mitt and my hand gets cold but it is worth it because the sandwich is really good. Meat and cheese and hot green things. Thank you Steve.

Skate skate skate.

I dont understand Steve asking who are the bad guys? You have to decide who the good guys are and help them. I remember thinking about him as Santas little brother but kids mostly want there own stuff—not other peoples. I would rather be Santa than Steve.

Maybe there is a way to make every body happy but I can not see it. If you can—well you are smarter than me. You and a lot of people.

IT IS NOT EASY TO GO HOME.

Youd think it would be but it is not. It is hard. I skate down 37. *Bridge to Canada 1 mile* says the first sine. Then *Bridge to Canada ½ Mile*. Then *Bridge To Canada 500 yards*. Then 200 yards. They really want you to know about it. There is no body on the road but me. The road is up hi and I can look down on a flat sheet of ice gleaming white in the nite with dark spots on it. The saint low rents. The dark spots are islands. Trees and rocks. Canada is on the other side of the river. The bridge goes across. There are US lites on this side and Canadian lites on the other side.

I follow the arrow and skate up to a little white booth in the middle of the road. *CUSTOMS* it says. Inside the booth theres an American flag and a picture of the president and the statu with her hand up. You know the 1. The man in the booth asks where my car is.

I dont have a car I say.

Are you looking for Brady or Alex? he asks.

I tell him I dont know Brady or Alex. I want to go to Canada I say. He nods. And now it gets hard. He puts his glove up to the hole in the window between us.

Pass port he says.

I dont have a pass port.

Then you cant visit another country.

I dont want to visit I say. I want to go home.

Give me some ID he says. And of course I cant.

I was kid napped I say. I escaped and now I am skating home.

He blinks a couple times. What? he says. When I start to tell him my story he makes a spitting noise. Get out of here kid he says. Go home.

He points behind me. The sine says *WELCOME TO THE UNITED STATES OF AMERICA*.

I dont live here I say. I live there.

I point across the river.

I am Canadian I say. I prove this by saying roof for him. And about and house. He makes the spitting noise again.

I have to get back soon—they will miss me in jail I say.

What? he says. He is paying attention now. What is this about a jail?

Its where I live I say.

Where were you last nite?

That was another jail I say. One of your jails.

Wait a second he says and picks up the phone.

I think what to tell him. I dont want to make things tuff for Bet. I explain about being in the rong jail. It looks like mine but it is not I say. I dont live there so I escaped and kept skating until my lace broke.

He nods at this but it is 2 late. It is all a mistake. I shuldnt of said anything. I feel a strong grab from behind. My arm is pinned by a guy with big ears and short hair. He marches me back down the road and off the bridge. His hands are bigger than my arm. There is a bilding at the side of the road—a blue trailer with an American flag over the door and a woman waiting for us inside. She is in uniform 2 and shes even bigger than the guy.

Hows our jail bird? she says to me.

Fine I say. Witch is not true. I am being polite. I am not fine. It wuld be hard to be less fine than I am rite now.

Actually I say I have been better.

The guy marches me over to the wall and says lean on this. So I do. And then he frisks me—checks my coat and chest and pockets and pant legs and everything.

What the heck? I ask.

The woman looms beside me like a cliff.

I am a victim I say. I was a hoss stage in your country and now I am trying to get home and you are not helping.

I explain about Vi and Lubor and Dusan—how they think that Grampa took there anthem and hid it some where and they want it and that is why they kid napped me.

My brother Spencer can tell you more. Call him I say. Or call Creekside jail where I live now. Call my prole officer. What is her name—Roz. I dont know her number but she is in Toronto. Or call my mom and dad I say. I can give you that number.

The 2 officers do not care. The guy holds up the nife that was in my coat pocket.

You are supposed to be in jail he says. You broke out and you are running away to Canada with a weapon and no ID. You are in trouble.

The woman officer leans down to speak close to me.

I dont trust you she says.

And that is when the party starts.

THE TRAILER IS NOT VERY BIG.

Apart from the room where we are talking theres an empty room like an office and that is all. I gess there is a bathroom but I never see it. The main room is crowded with the 3 of us in it so you can imagine what happens when 1 2 3 6 10 more people show up. I dont know how many it is actually but it is a lot and they all show up together. In a minit the place is jammed like an ants nest. People shout Happy Holidays Brady and Alex and pat the officers on the back. I dont know who is who but they are both popular.

There are bottles and glasses and snacks and a music player. It is a party. The woman officer trys to stop it but she cant. Nobody listens when she says go home. Nobody cares.

Its deadest time of the year! shouts one guy. Nothing is going to happen tonite!

He is beanpole thin. I am not fat but I am 2wice as big as him. He is thin and stands strait with brite red hair. He looks like a match. Its party time! he shouts.

Somebody standing near the woman officer gives her a drink. The guy officer already has a drink. The bean pole beside me gives me a drink. I say thank you. He pats me on the back.

I'm Kenton he says. His breath smells like peaches. Im Bunny I say and he laffs like I have made a joke. When he asks how I am doing I say Not fine. I am not polite any more.

Kenton laffs again and asks how I know Brady and Alex. We all went to school together he says. Perivale Tech—down hi way 37 there. Brady and Alex are so strait now he says. Cops would you beleeve it? They were crazy back in school he says. Theyd go to Canada and start fites. One nite they both ended up in jail.

I think they want to put me in jail now I say.

He laffs. Everything I say he laffs at.

Your funny! he says. He pats me some more. This is a funny guy! he tells the room.

My drink smells like peaches. I cant tell if it is bad or good but I have another sip. Yeah it is pretty bad.

Kenton tells me to drink up. The party goes on. The music is a song every body knows and they start singing and dancing. I can not help dancing along. I do not know the song but the trailer is rocking and I have to move to stay on my feet.

Kenton notices.

Hey you have skates on! Your a riot! he says.

I came on my skates I say.

The world is tilted at a funny angle. I take off my coat and hang on to it. I dont want any more peach stuff.

Kenton nods like Aha. You skated over—thats why you are in trouble he says.

The guy officer comes over. Brady or Alex. He takes a drink from his glass.

Who are you? he says to me.

He takes another drink.

Ive seen you befor he says. But I cant think where.

He shakes his head and finishes his glass. He wanted to arrest me and now he doesnt remember who I am. I start to laff. Kenton is all ready laffing.

This guy is the funniest! he says. Say something Bunny—say something funny.

Funny Bunny says the customs officer. Funny Bunny—yeah thats pretty good.

And I didnt even say anything.

Are you Brady? I ask him. Or Alex?

He doesnt know who I am and I dont know who he is. We all laff.

See! Kenton puts his arm around my sholders. Bunny is a riot! he says.

The air is starting to swim. The music is loud and we are jumping up and down to dance. The floor is moving like an earth quake. Alex or Brady staggers. I cant tell if I am dancing or not. I am sort of jumping. My arms and legs move on there own.

Alex or Brady moves off to find another drink. The trailer shifts and sinks to one side. At least I think it does. The pole with the flag on it falls over. The song ends.

Where are you skating to Bunny? says Kenton.

Canada.

I know a secret way to Canada he says. No customs or anything.

What way? I ask. Where?

We used to—Kenton starts but the music comes up and everyone goes back to jumping and I cant hear the rest.

What? I say.

When we were in school says Kenton. We did it all the time. Theres a way down from up here he says. There are yellow stickers on the trees to mark the path.

I dont know what he is talking about.

What path? I say.

He looks past my sholder. I feel a hand grab my upper arm. It is the other officer, the woman—Brady or Alex.

Ive been keeping an eye on you she says. What are you talking about?

Ive been telling Bunny about the path down to the river.

No Kenton! she says. He cant go to Canada. Hes a criminal. He broke out of jail. He has to stay here.

What? says Kenton. Is this true?

Sort of.

You are joking—rite?

No joke says Brady or Alex. She drags me away. The music is on and people are drinking and bouncing.

I still dont trust you she says. And I dont want Kenton helping you. Come here.

I have to go with her. She is so big she is like a troll. Her hand is a hook. She pulls me to the other room of the trailer and locks me in.

The good news is I am not with Vi and the other kid nappers. But I am still locked up in an empty room with no window or telephone or chairs. It is not as cold as the basement in the Newman house but it is pretty cold. I zip up my coat and slump until I am sitting on the plastic carpet. The music gets louder and the floor bounces under me when everybody starts dancing. I sit with my legs strait out. My skates are done up.

I REMEMBER GOING SKATING WITH MY SCHOOL

back when I was in grade 3. The rink was down King Street and we walked. We had buddys and we had to hold hands. Nancy from the front row picked me for her buddy and then got in a fite with Rich witch I didnt understand at first—I thot Rich wanted to be my buddy 2. But no. He wanted to be Nancys buddy and he didnt know why she picked me.

It all came out while we were skating. I was practicing turns crossing my legs over and Nancy was saying Wow and Way to go Bunny. Rich tripped me as I past him so I was lying on the ice on my back looking up at the 2 of them.

Hes stupid said Rich.

Meaning me.

Hes the stupidest kid in the class.

I dont care said Nancy.

You shuld be my walk buddy said Rich. Were both smart. You will be my buddy on the way home he said.

No I wont she said and pushed him. He bent in the middle like a folding chair and went down so there were 2 of us on the ice. Nancy put her hand out to me and helped me stand up. And we went back to our skating.

I think that was the first time I new about myself. Not because Rich said I was a dummy—I heard that a lot. But Nancy didnt say no I wasnt stupid. She just said she didnt mind. So I figured that I really was stupid and that it wasnt that big a deal.

My snow pants made that *zoop zoop* sound when I walked back to school beside Nancy. I wonder what happened to her. We were in different classes in grade 4 and then she moved away. She had curly black hair and glasses with a strap to hold them on and no fear. Sometimes the important people in your life are not there for long.

I AM SLEEPY

and I drift from thinking about Nancy into a dream of falling. When I wake up its true. Theres a cracking sound and I end up on my side and theres something rong with the customs trailer. I wasnt sure befor but I am now. The floor has dropped away from the bottom of the outside wall. I can see a strip of nite and feel a cold wind.

The music on the other side of the door is loud. There is still bumping going on—the dancing. I am cold because of the open strip of wall. I put on my glove and mitt. I think about standing up and shouting for help but a voice inside me says wait.

You know that voice. The corner of the floor drops again. It is angled down and I am sliding toward the crack.

Wait says the voice.

There is another crack and the floor falls out. I end up on the hill under the trailer with a sore bum from the drop. It hurts like when you go over a bump on a tobogan witch is what the floor of my room is now—a tobogan.

I slide down the hill on it. I look up and see the lites of the trailer behind me and the bridge over my head. I hit a tree root and the wood floor cracks but the plastic carpet keeps going with me on it so I go even faster than befor. Plastic is my magic carpet. I just miss a tree and then an other. The sky is clear and the moon is mostly full—like a Ritz cracker with a bite out of it—so there are clear shadows on the snow. When the moon lite hits the tree ahead of me there is a flash from a yellow sticker. Farther down I pass another flash. This is Kentons path. I gess I am going the best way down. I stick out my hands to steer but the path is pretty smooth. I only have time for 1 or 2 breaths and then the carpet flys over the bank of the river and I land on my bum witch hurts some more. The ice is flat and smooth so I skid and spin for a while befor I can roll off the plastic and stand up. I have to blink. The moon is brite and the ice and snow are white all around me and Canada is dead ahead.

A minit ago US customs had me locked in a room and in trouble. A lot can happen in a minit. Holy crap says a voice. No this is not the voice you trust. This is my voice. I am talking out loud.

I never skated away on a river befor. That song is in my head as I take off. The ice is smooth and the wind has blown off most of the snow. The skating is great. Left glide rite glide left glide. I hear a wolf howling. I gess he is howling at the moon. It sounds erie and cool.

I pass an island with a tree and nothing else—a desert island from a comic strip. There shuld be a ragged guy throwing a bottle with a note in it only that wuldnt work because it is winter. I pass an island with more trees and another island with no trees at all. I hear a booming sound come from underneath me and I stop. Is the ice splitting? Is there a hole ahead? I dont want to fall in. The ice feels strong under my skates but I watch care fully for a hole—witch is how I come to see the foot prints in a patch

of snow. There is a rapper beside the foot prints—
shiny paper that looks like it was on a hamburger.
I remember what Kenton said about Alex and Brady
crossing over to Canada to have fites when they were
in school. It seems I am not the only 1 on the river
tonite. I look all around but I cant see any body or
any other hint of any body. The rapper is from befor.
I skate and skate. I hear a train whistle a long way
away and then the wolf agane. I see a shadow on a
patch of snow ahead of me and look up to see an owl
floating toward the US. It mite not be an owl but
I dont know any other nite birds.

Left glide rite glide. Deep breath. Glide.

River skating is better than a rink. I feel this
amazing sense of freedom. The open—the empty—
the world—the ALL of it. Being alone in a big place
takes you away—like you can float off and look at
yourself from a distance. Here I am in my little life
trying to deal with my troubles. Some people are
worrying about me and some are helping me and
some are making it hard for me and all the time
theres this—this—this gigantic ALL all around me.
It makes me feel small but also grate full. Maybe not
grate full xactly—maybe more like you see how awe

some everything is. My family only goes to church 2wice a year and I dont pay much attention xept for the singing and if there are donuts in the church base-ment after words so I am not talking about God here. I dont know anything about God. But as I am skating late at nite across this river that goes forever and the ice smooth and fresh and the moon shining down I am like—wow.

Until I put my foot thru the ice. Then I stop thinking big thots and go back to worrying.

I AM WET UP TO MY NEE.

I mean knee. Mr Wing made lists of tricky words for me. One of them was words with *x* at the start like xplain—witch you dont spell that way but I sometimes do. An other list was words with letters you dont say. Knee was on that list along with knit and know. And there were lots of *w* words. I still get mixed up. I dont rite knee very much. I mean write. I am sitting on the ice with my leg in the water. I try to pull my leg out but the hole is the wrong shape and I cant.

Wrong is another tricky word. Sometimes I get it and sometimes I dont. Wrong and write. I try again, standing up so I can pull harder. My foot wont fit.

I watched a movy about survival and it was pretty scary. This plane went down in the mountains and it was winter outside and it got gross. Spencer was with me in the living room and he kept talking about camera angles and how great this shot was and all the time I was thinking that these guys were eating each other. Ew.

There is nobody for me to eat out here on the ice but I have to get out of the water fast. And then I have to get warm. The movy made that clear.

I wish I was in the living room with Spencer now. I wuld let him watch whatever he wanted. I wuld even make him a sandwich witch I dont normally do.

The ice is thicker than a thick book. The hole is cut rite thru it. Somebody must of done that witch means that they stopped here and needed water so they culd fish or drink or I dont know. Whatever you use water for. Probly not to have a bath. People were here. Maybe the hamburger eater was here.

Hello! I shout. It is the first thing I have said in a while.

Help! I shout. The wind takes my voice away.

Overhead is the bitten out moon and more stars than I have ever seen. I find the pail with Orvils special star somewhere in it but I dont care about north rite now. I want to get out.

I hop around the hole slowly trying to get my foot in the same shape as when it fit in. Trying not to worry about my shivers and my foot feeling num. There! No not quite. Then the ice makes that booming sound and the hole shifts a bit and my skate pops out.

I'm okay! What a relief.

All this time I am looking down at the ice and my skate. I am consentrating—I think that is it. Paying attention. So when my foot is free and I look up and see the wolf rite there beside me I am surprised. I did not know it was there.

WOLVES ARE NOT WHAT YOU THINK.

Sure they are tuff looking and they have teeth and claws and all but they are not super bad guys. They are not going to attack you and carry you away unless you live in a ferry tail. Mostly they are shy. The TV show I saw was clear about this—nobody gets killed by wolves. Nobody. You are way more likely to get hurt by a cow than a wolf. Cows are mean.

So I am surprised to see this wolf but not worryed at all. OK maybe a bit.

Hi there I say. I test my wet leg. It squelches but it still works. There is ice on my skate blade. I bend down to slide it off. The wolf is pacing a few feet away from me.

Good dog. That sounds wrong as soon as I say it. Wolfs are like dogs but they are not dogs. No way is this a dog.

I think about Little Red Riding Hood. How old is she—like 8 or 9? Just a kid. This wolf would take her and her gramma easy.

I have the ice off my skate blade now. I am shivering pretty good. I have to get out of here. My foot is soaked but I can still skate.

Bye bye! I say and start off slowly. The wolf moves in front of me. If I keep skating I will hit it so I stop. The wolf stares at me. I take off to the left thinking I can go around the wolf. It moves again. Without trying really hard it gets ahead of me. It can move faster than me. Its pads and claws work better than my tired legs and dull skates. But why is it doing this? Does it think we are playing a game?

Go away! I say.

Stupid wolf! I say.

The wolf looks at me and yawns wide then turns away and lifts a leg to pee.

I am not going to let this animal stop me. I have to get to the other side of the river. I head a bit left and so does the wolf. Then I push off hard as tho I am going to go farther left only I cut back insted. Its a fake—like I am playing hockey and the wolf is a defense man. I am past him! The wolf falls for my fake and there is only 1 more island befor I get to Canada.

I am heading a little to the rite of where I was befor but so what. The wolf is running 2 but he is not trying to get ahead of me any more. Now we are running in the same direction. What do they call that—paranormal? No thats a movie. Something like that. I know the word. I will think of it later. I keep an eye on the wolf and at the same time try to watch out for more holes in the ice.

Left. Glide. Deep breath. Rite. Glide.

Im tired and woozy from all I have been doing—getting in trouble and escaping and drinking that funny peach stuff and escaping again and freezing my leg—witch maybe xplains why I start to see things. Maybe I am getting sick. But I cant help what I see. The sky off to the left now has lines of ripples running across it. Rippling pink and green lites—what is that about? Am I crazy? And its brite out—almost as brite as day. I can see the wolf clearly. He has long legs and a thin body. Hes gray mostly with a black splotch on his sholder and another on his head like hes wearing a black scarf and hat. Have I said Im not afraid of the wolf? Thats not quite it. I dont think hes going to eat me but theres something about him. The way he lopes along kind of sideways. The way he checks me out and then shakes his head. We are still running parallel him and me. Thats the word—the same way but not touching. Hes tired like me. His mouth is open so he can pant. It looks like he is smiling at me. Does he like me or not? Not wuld be my gess.

The last island is small and roundish and it doesnt stick out of the ice very far. I pass close enuff to the island that I see the small green tree leaning over so far its branches are trapped in the ice. Shadowy and secret looking—and even more so in the pink and green lite.

Is it really pink and green? I blink. Yup.

I take a deep breath and get ready to head across the last bit of river. Thats when I see the jim bag—sorry gym bag. Its dark and its got handles and it is sitting in the shadows of the over hanging tree. I wuldnt of seen it if I had not been skating so close to the island. Huh I think. I dont want to grab it. Its probly yucky and I all ready have a gym bag. I take a stride toward shore and hear my name.

Bernard.

No mistaking—its as clear as clear. I stop short in a flurry of ice specks and look around. Nobody calls me Bernard. Spencer called me Bunny when he was a baby and it has been my name ever since.

Bernard.

There it is again. But theres no body around. Who is talking to me? The only person who ever called me Bernard was Grampa. He didnt like the name Bunny. I am used to hearing my name in Grampas voice and I do now. I gess its coming from inside me. I do feel kinda crazy come to think of it. Not bad or sick—just crazy. Bigger than normal if you know what I mean. My mood matches the sky witch is dancing with curtins of lite now.

Go and see Bernard.

Definitely Grampas voice but it is not coming from me. My mouth is shut—has been shut all along.

Grampa is that you? I say. Witch is stupid because it cant be Grampa. But who else sounds like him? Who else is around? Who else can I see? Just the wolf who has stopped running and is sitting down looking at me hard. He opens his mouth.

Yes Bernard says Grampas voice. The wolf closes his mouth.

Hoo boy.

SO I AM CRAZY.

Thats all I can think. Grampa can not be the wolf and he is not talking to me. I close my eyes tite. Maybe the wolf will be gone when I open them again.

Nope.

Hurry Bernard.

His mouth moves again. And now that I come to think of it the wolfs gray like Grampa. And thin like Grampa. And Grampa wore a dark hat. Oh well I think. I will have to get used to being crazy. Whatever. I am still feeling hi and lite and I am long past being weirded out.

Go and see said Grampa the wolf.

I am not sure of anything but I skate over to the gym bag. The ice is bumpy near the island. I look back.

Is this what you mean? I ask out loud.

The wolf yawns and ducks his head witch culd be a nod. Okay then. I pick up the gym bag. Its crappy and old and faded blu. The handles are cracked plastic. Inside is smelly—looks full of towels and stuff. I zip it back up fast.

Can we go now? I say.

I figure the wolf is coming with me. I dont try to change direction and lose him. I know I cant. We go together—me and Grampa the wolf.

I remember my cousins fiting about Grampa last week. Was it last week? Whenever. At the cottage when we found all his secret stuff. This may be a chance to ask him.

Were you really a spy back a long time ago? I ask the wolf. When you were flying around the world did you do stuff like James Bond? I ask.

The wolf looks at me. Does he nod again? I feel stupid but I keep on anyway.

Some guys think you have there anthem Grampa I say. Did you take it? Was that part of your spying? These same guys kid napped me. They are bad guys rite? Rite Grampa?

I dont know what I am asking. My problem is that I dont know who the good guys are. Kid napping is bad but so is stealing an anthem. Maybe Grampa was a bad guy. I dont know how you tell.

Also my problem is that I am talking to a wolf.

He doesnt answer.

Im getting close to the shore. My strokes are shorter and harder and my gliding is not as smooth. Its not as brite ether. A long ribbon of green pulls across the sky with a tail of sparks behind it. Theres a ripple and a flash—and then nothing. The sky show is over. The nite looks normal again as I glide the last few feet and step up onto the bank. This side of the river is flatter than the American side. I can walk up. The bag swings in my hand. Theres a road near the edge of the river. A pick up truck goes by. Head lites blaze for a second and then are gone. I pick my way over icy rocks so I dont wreck my skates any more than they are already wrecked.

Wreck is an other of Mr Wings *w* words.

Its the same stuff as across the river but it feels different to me. Trees and rocks and snow and snow. And ice. And snow. Canada. I am a long way from home but I am home.

Bernard.

The familiar voice is quiet but clear. The wolf stands in a clump of trees. The black cap on his gray head looks very much like Grampas beret.

Take care he says.

Whats happening now? I ask.

I have to go he says. Take care of whats in the bag and take care of yourself. Will you do that Bernard?

Wait I say. Dont go.

The wolf turns back to look at me over his sholder. I swear hes ticked off. A very Grampa look.

Will you do it? he asks. When I say yes he nods.

Thats your job he says. Do it. You are a good guy Bernard.

How did he know I was wondering about good guys and bad guys? But befor I can ask anything about him he leaps into the darkness and is gone.

Do your job. Thanks Grampa. Like I need telling. I know I have to call Spencer so he doesnt worry about me. And I have to get back to Creekside. These are my jobs.

I dont know about Grampa being a spy for the bad guys or the good guys. I asked but he didnt say. Is it my job to find out? I dont know how Id do it. Its the sort of thing DJ wuld be good at. Or Steve or Adam. These guys wuld have ideas. They wuld call people and go places and do things. Maybe Webb wuld have an idea. Or the new guy—I really shuld know his name—hes my cousin. Anyway I dont have any ideas at all.

Does Grampa care about spying any more? He seems pretty happy being a wolf. If that was him. And if it wasnt then Im crazy and Grampa is dead and he doesnt care about anything.

Do your job. OK I got it.

I dont know witch way to go so I pick left. I always pick left when I dont know. The road goes up hill to a bigger road and then I have to pick again. So I make another left and keep going. Skating is harder than it was. My blades are dull. Also there is ice on the side of the road but not in the middle. The plows have gone out. So I am having trouble keeping going.

The strange lites in the sky are gone. Were they real or part of a dream or those things you see when you are crazy sick?

Push left. Glide. Push rite. Glide.

Do your job still makes sense.

THE RIVER IS BESIDE ME AND THE MOON IN FRONT.

The road is more normal looking. The letters and number on the sines for instants. Beside the road there are posts with yellow reflecting things on the top. I didnt see those in the US. I shuld of known rite away that I wasnt in Canada. I must be even stupider than they say.

Theres nobody around—no cars or lites or houses. I totally can not find the north pointing star. I know its small and near the stars that look like a pail and I can not see that ether. I feel like I am looking thru the telly scope again and not seeing whatever it was Gally Layo saw. Moons? Moons. I dunno.

I am sick of carrying this crappy gym bag. One of the handles has broken and it is dangling from my hand. The wolf said to take care of the bag but hes not around. Hes probly not even real. Now that Ive escaped from Skrillex and Brady and Alex and Vi and Lubor and America—now that I am almost home—I figure I must of been dreaming when I talked to the wolf and thot he was Grampa. Dreaming or what do you call it—seeing things. So I dont need to do what he said.

Theres something heavy in the bag—like a stone or something. I feel it moving as the bag swings. A thot comes out of no place.

What if its money?

Now I go back to thinking that wolf Grampa is real. Maybe he led me to the gym bag so Id find money inside. I found a back pack full of money last summer. Thats 1 of the reasons I am in Creekside now—the money. Also the dead body. Dont ask—its a long story.

How much do you trust Grampa? Spencer wasnt talking about Grampa the wolf but its still a good question.

Anyway I dont throw away the gym bag. I keep skating and when I come to the next street lite I stop and open it. I am all ready thinking of what to do with the money. Spencer can have something for his camera and Benj at Creekside can have a poster of the Maple Leafs. He is a big fan. Id like to help Bet but I cant think how. And you cant help every body. Sorry Steve you cant. I shuld give some of the money to my cousins. Or maybe we shuld just split it since were all grandsons. Thinking of Grampa I want to find out if there is a wolf shelter or wolf fund or something. I bet there is. Some of the money shuld go there to say thank you.

By now I am almost sure about whats in the bag—the only question is how much. A hundred dollars? A thousand? A billion? All rite not a billion but it culd still be a lot. So I am pretty disappointed when I push aside the towelly things and a small clear plastic bag of cereal and find the sleeping baby.

Really? Yeah. Small and rinkly and curled up with a thum in its mouth. The gym bag is a baby bag. The towel things are some kind of diaper.

I look around half expecting to see Grampa so I can ask him what I am supposed to do now. Cause I have no idea. Im a kid—15 last birthday and not very smart. What do I know about babys? Nothing. I mean I know where they come from but thats all.

Who wants a baby? I would rather have money.

I can see the little sholders moving when the baby shivers. It turns its head and yawns and then goes back to sleep. It has a hat on and mitts and a scarf and bootys and all but its cold. Well of course it is. The bag was on the ice. The babys been outside a long time. An hour? 2 hours? A long time.

So the first thing I have to do is get the baby warm. I zip up the bag and hold it to me. I dont want the other handle to break now. I look around for head lites.

Nothing coming. Drat.

I skate care fully and think about ways to warm up the baby. There are no cars and no houses. Can I start a fire? No. What can I do? The warmest place I can reach rite now is—well—me. I cant give the baby my coat but I can put it inside my coat. I stop again. How to do this? My brain is working as fast as it can. The best way seems to be for me to wear the gym bag like a front pack with the handles around my sholders and the bag on my chest and my coat over everything. So I try that. Now my body heat will warm up the bag and the baby. The broken handle means the bag hangs off to my left. So what. I zip my coat back sup and go.

Where is every body?

I skate care fully. Push left. Glide a bit. Push rite. Glide a bit more.

The road ends at a cross roads. Left wuld take me back to the river so I go rite for a change. Still no houses or farms. Canada is a big empty country. You forget that when you are driving around. Try skating and you will see it is full of no people. You will see how far it is between places.

The baby is awake. I can feel it move around and hear it breathing. And there is a car coming! Its behind me. A car with a reason to be out late at nite. Some body to save me and the baby. I turn and jump and wave both arms. Stop! I shout.

The car is not slowing down.

Please stop!

The car zooms past. Tail lights glow red for a minit and then disappear.

The baby starts crying.

ITS COMING FROM UNDER MY COAT.

The gym bag bumps against my hart. I feel the baby going *uhh* when it breaths in and then *mew mew* and then *uhh* again. The crying is not loud but I cant miss it. Its coming from inside me. Its like I am crying.

There there I say.

The baby does not stop. *Uhh. Mew. Uhh. Mew mew.* Great. This is great. I am having a wonderful time.

Push. Glide. Think. What could be rong with the baby? It is not as cold any more so its probly hungry. When I wake up from a nap Im hungry. Come to think of it I am hungry rite now. I think about foods I like. A grill cheese sandwich. Cereal.

I remember the oat meal cookys at Steves house and I feel a bit like crying myself. Theres a small blu sine at the side of the road. 3731279. Whatever that means. Snow and trees and dark all around.

There are cheerios in the gym bag. The baby can eat those but not yet. It is 2 cold to eat in the middle of the road. Tuff luck baby. Keep crying. I will stop the next car that comes by if I have to stand in the middle of the road to do it.

Push and glide.

I have not herd any crying in a while. Is the baby back to sleep? Maybe. I am not tired any more. I am hungry and worryed.

Another blu sine. 3771592.

Still nothing from the baby. Not even breathing in—I can not feel or hear the *uhhh*. I stop at the next street lite and open my coat and unzip the gym bag a bit more. The baby looks up at me and opens its mouth but no noise comes out. Is it 2 weak to cry? Wow. This is not good. I can hear Grampas voice telling me to look after what is in the bag. But how? Nobody is around. There is only me and the street lites and miles and miles of empty road. And trees and snow. I do not know where the hi way is or the next town or the hospital or anything. I am lost. I am letting the baby down. And Grampa.

I need an idea. Smart people get them all the time. Spencer does I know. Come on brain—dont fail me now.

3779912.

What are these sines about? They dont show turn-offs—theres no where to go. Snow and forest is all I can see. I whack at the sine with my mitt fist. Im upset and angry. The feeling sits inside me like that big bite of peanut butter you cant get down. Its nothing to do with Grampa or rite and rong. Its not about Vi this time. Im angry because the baby is weak. Im angry I cant make it better. Im angry at me I gess. Hitting the sine is my kind of idea—stupid. Xept that when I nock over the sine it hits the pole behind it and I see something.

Not nock—knock. Its another of Mr Wings tricky spelling words for me. Know knock knee write wrong. After Christmas he wants me to learn about commas and stuff. I told him you dont need commas for anything and he says yes you do. He is wrong.

The pole behind the sine has a box on it. I didnt see it befor. And when I step forward and wipe the snow off the box I see a name.

GOYETTE.

Its a male box. Witch means theres a house back there in the snowy forest. I decide to find it. Is that an idea? Not really. But its what Im going to do. I hop-walk off the road and up thru the snow bank. The trees are mostly ever green. I start moving left and rite as I go forward. I dont know where the house is and I dont want to walk past it.

I am thinking that those blu numbers must all be house numbers. There are a few houses along this road. If I was smarter I culd of figured this out and Id be inside all ready. But theres no point in thinking about that. I am here now.

The ground feels different under my skates. Little stones. A lot of them. A drive way. I follow it up hill and around a bend and there is the house—dark against the star brite sky.

Hang in there baby I say out loud.

The drive way loops up to the door. No lites any where and no foot prints in the snow xept mine. I hop-walk to the door and pound on it but I dont wait long because this is an emergency and there are no rules in emergency. Beside the door is a small window. I smash it with a kick from my skate and reach in and around to open the door from the inside.

HELLO! I SHOUT.

No anser. I turn on some lites and look around for the thing where you set how hot you want the place to be. Its in the living room. I smile at the *whoosh* sound from the furnace when I turn up the heat. Its great to be inside and walking around in socks and to feel warm air on me. I stuff a kitchen towel in the broken window. In a few minits it is warm enuff to take off my coat. I put the gym bag down on a chair. The baby inside stares up at me with eyes like black beads.

Hi there I say as I lift it out.

Not that I like the baby. I dont. But I dont want it to die on me. So I act frendly and tickle it in the tummy like people do. The baby does not want to sit up so I put it on my lap facing out and use my arm as a seat belt to hold it safe. It is bigger than a loaf of bread but not much. A big loaf of bread. I find the cheerios and offer them. The baby looks away. And then it looks at me. I can read its mind. I know what it is feeling. I am feeling it 2.

Thirsty.

I take the baby with me to the kitchen sink and run some water. The baby perks up. But now we run into trouble. There are no bottles or baby cups. All this water and no way to get it to the baby. The next 5 minits are almost funny they are so awful. I can not get the water into the baby. I can get close—I can get a glass rite up to the babys mouth—but close is not good enuff. I can not get the baby to drink. It trys to drink from the glass. Gosh it trys. But it cant. It moves its mouth and gasps and chokes and spills and almost dies. Its not fair. I want the baby to drink and it wants to drink. We are both on the same side and we are losing.

The baby is so thirsty and mad it cries. I know how it feels. I feel like crying myself.

I get an idea. I put the baby on the floor on its back and neel over it and pour water into its mouth like you pour into a glass. This is a bad idea. Lots of spilling and coffing head turning and arm waving. Everything gets wet. I wipe up and sit the baby on my lap and try again.

Arrrg. Nope.

I drink myself to show the baby how you do it. I only mean to take a sip but the waters so good I cant help drinking the hole glass. I lean over the sink and pour another glass with 1 hand. I hold the baby with the other. I hear loud sucking noises. Hah! The towel I used to wipe up the water is on my sholder and the baby has the end in its mouth. It is drinking. I pull out the towel and wet it again. The baby goes back to drinking.

Hah! Hah! We have a system.

My relief is like dropping a heavy suit case.

The house phone doesnt work. I tryed it first thing. The Goyettes must be away for a while and turned off there phone. Thats why there are no cars or lites and the drive way is snowed over. The Goyettes are in Florida or Cuba getting sun tans.

In a few minits the place really starts to heat up. The baby is still drinking. I take off some of its close. It has a lot of black hair. A lot. When I pull off the hat

it is like opening a joke can with snakes in it. Boom!
Hair. I have to laff.

I wonder what her name is? Or his. It looks like a
girl with all that hair but I dont know for sure. And
I dont wanna find out. For me it is an it.

It stops drinking long enuff to eat the hole bag
of cheerios and it is still hungry when they are gone.
It looks at the empty bag. I know that look. I look at
my empty plate that way sometimes. I wet the towel
for the 300th time and the baby goes back to drinking.

Theres no cereal in the kitchen but I hunt around
the shelves and find a can of pasta with a pop top.
Woo hoo! Good stuff—tomato sauce and cheese.
I can eat it cold and so can the baby. We share. The
baby eats from my spoon. When I spill it licks my
finger. We finish pretty quick and the baby falls asleep
in my lap befor I even know. I put it on the couch and
cover it up and think—what the hell?

I havent had time yet. But now that we are warm
and safe and fed and the baby is sleeping I can
wonder—what the hell is going on?

There are 2 parts to my what the hell. The first
part has to do with the baby. How did it end up on the
ice? Who leaves a baby on the ice? Not mom and dad

—at least not this babys mom and dad. They care about it or they wuldnt of packed diapers and cheerios. So who? A bad guy trying to kill the baby? That doesnt sound rite. Who hates a baby that much?

I dont know the anser. So much for that part of my what the hell.

The second part has to do with me. Maybe I got kid napped so some place could get back the anthem that Grampa stole. But what about Grampa the wolf steering me across the ice to the gym bag and telling me to take care of what was in it? How much do I beleeve? What the hell is going on with me? I dont know the anser to this ether. But there is the baby making a little snuffy noise in its sleep. I cant deny that. Its totally real. So the rest is something I just have to take on faith for now. Chance. Grampa. Whatever.

Now the baby makes a noise. I know the noise and so do you. Yah that noise. It is a funny noise when you make it with your lips or under your arm pit—but the baby is not making the noise under its arm pit.

Oh.

The baby frowns and grunts and turns over in its sleep. Theres the noise again. The baby has had a lot to drink and eat and it is ready to—it is starting to—to—oh no.

Oh no no!

The noise goes on and on and on. And on.

And still there is more noise and more—more. Its epic. My jaw drops open and stays there. I dont know wether to scream or laff or start clapping. I am impressed. The baby sounds like it is digging to China or firing a rocket at the moon—and it sleeps thru the hole thing.

I dont want to talk about the next ten minits. The smell. The noise. The filth. The amazing amazing filth. Maybe not as bad as being kid napped and locked up in a cold basement but no fun. Trust me.

About half way thru the front door opens.

SUSAN DEAR–ARE YOU THERE?

The voice is old sounding. A woman is in the hall. I dont anser because I am not Susan and because I am on the kitchen floor on my nees finishing up with the baby—who is a girl by the way. I can not tell you how yucky it all is. Its like the baby exploded. The only clean part of her is her hair. Everything else is going to have to go in the wash or the garbage. I reach into the gym bag for diaper number 4.

Susan is Susan Goyette I gess—this is her house.

Knees not nees.

The lady in the hall says ahem. Shes polite.

I saw the lites on and the broken window and I wondered she says a bit louder.

I wonder what the babys name is? Her hair is soft. Her skin is warmer than it was.

Is everything all rite? asks the lady. Answer me. And what on earth is that smell?

She shows up in the kitchen doorway. I am not surprised by her parka or boots or white hair or rinkles. Im surprised by the rifle tho. She points it at me pretty steddy. A tuff lady.

What are you doing? She starts to say and then stops when she sees the baby and the mess. Its easy to see what I am doing. There are little close and diapers all over the floor.

I say hi and tell her my name and that I am sorry for breaking in. It was an emergency I say—the baby needed help.

So you are not a robber.

Well I did take a can of pasta I say. She smiles and lowers the gun and tells me her name is Katy. With a *Y* she says witch she doesnt have to because how else am I going to spell it?

Hi Katy I say.

All this time the baby is sleeping and stinking and I am fumbling with diapers and wipes and close. Katy asks do I want any help and I say yes so fast she hasnt finished asking me yet. Yes yes please I say. In about 5 minits she has the baby clean and in a blanket and the dirty close in a washing machine in the basement. She is like a hurricane of busy.

I go to the bathroom and clean up.

What is her name? Katy asks me while the close are washing. We are sitting in the living room.

Who? I ask.

The baby—the little girl with the hair. What is her name?

I dont know I say.

Who is she?

I dont know.

Katy frowns and puffs on her cigaret. She smokes all the time. When she finishes 1 she lites an other 1.

Whats going on Bunny? she asks.

She is smart and tuff and old and full of energy. Can I trust her? Can she help me?

I find myself telling her my story. Not Grampa the wolf but most of the other stuff. The baby close go in the dryer and Im still talking. Katy has her head tilted so the smoke doesnt go into her eyes. When I am done she nods a bit and says good.

Good? I say. Whats good?

You are she says. You are doing the rite thing.

Even tho I dont know whats going on?

Knowing whats going on is over rated she says. You know whats important.

She pats my arm. For all that she is old and smoking like a bonfire she reminds me of Nancy in grade 3. I feel better because of her. The bell dings and the dryer is done.

KATY GOES OUT TO HER TRUCK

while I dress the baby in her snow suit and hat. Blah blah blah she says and grabs my nose. I give her another drink from the wet towel and then it is time to go.

Dont point that at me says Katy.

Sorry.

She takes the rifle from me and throws it in the backseat of the truck. I sit in the front with the baby in my lap. She looks around and grabs everything she can. Mostly me.

Katy drives off slowly.

Were you really going to shoot me? I ask. If I was a robber.

I told Susan Id watch her place while she was away.

And you do what you say youll do.

Well sure she says.

Its late and the road is empty and wild looking. Pine trees make it look even wilder. There is no town—only more sines with numbers. The truck smells of smoke. The cigaret buts in the ash tray look like an under sea animal—a coral or sponge with white things sticking up.

So you wuld of shot me? I ask.

I was going to try to scare you she says. But if you wouldnt be scared then yeah Id of pulled the trigger.

What if you missd?

You dont miss with a shot gun she says.

Katy has the radio on. The announcer guy has a gaspy voice and he says O boy a lot.

Less than 24 hours from now the ball will drop and the new year will begin he says. Then he starts talking about Aiden Tween who is in Toronto. O boy what a hart throb he says. Katy turns off the radio.

Cant stand that guy she says.

Aiden Tween?

Well yeah him 2. But I was talking about that radio host. He sounds like he has found a cure for cancer when hes giving a traffic report.

You know Aiden Tween rite? The singer? You baby you baby you baby are the 1 for me—that guy. Hes famous. The hair the pointing finger the screaming fans. Hes my age witch means we shuld have a lot in common—only we dont.

Katy pulls into the parking lot of the police station. It is near the 401 hi way and is the only big bilding I have seen in Canada so far. She shuts off the engine and we walk in together.

Your wearing skates? she says.

Yeah.

Rented eh? I see the number.

She opens the door for me and the baby. I click and clump across the floor of the station.

The sarjent behind the desk is yelling into 2 phones at once. She has 1 in her hand and 1 lying open in front of her.

There is a table and chairs near the front door—a waiting area. The magazine on the table has a picture of a guy with his hand in his shirt on the cover. Napoleon it says. He was a long time ago but the magazine looks old enuff to have gossip about him like he was Aiden Tween. Crazy Napoleon—whats he up to now?

I sit down and keep the baby in my lap. She pulls off her hat and drops it rite away.

I dont care Stevens! says the sarjent into her hand phone. Command center is breathing down my neck. Its been 5 hours now. Make up another search team and go to the customs shed.

Katy walks over to the desk and goes ahem. The sarjent puts up her free hand like a stop sine to say Wait a minit.

And bring search lites! she says. You can run them off the car batteries. Come on Stevens. Do it now!

The minit the sarjent gets off this phone the 1 on the desk rings. She leans over and says Yes sir and No sir a lot and then goodbye sir.

There is a moment of silence.

Hello says Katy who is still standing beside the desk. The sarjents hand phone rings.

Itll be a second she says to Katy and then says Yes into the phone.

Katy goes outside for a smoke. Its been a couple minits since her last.

The baby likes dropping her hat. And pulling my nose. These are her things to do. I poke her in the stomach and she giggles. I giggle back.

Not that I like her—I dont. Just a baby. Geez.

The sarjent is yelling into the phone again. Dont talk to me about how cold it is! she shouts. Its winter out there. Why do you think were all worried about little Adeline?

The baby stands up strait. Looks past my sholder. And speaks for the first time.

Ad she says.

I dont know what she means. The word sounds like dad. Does she think Im her dad?

I give her that hat. She drops it.

Ad she says again.

The sarjent closes the phone she is talking into. Sorry she says to Katy who is back from her smoke now. This is a very busy nite. Theres a lost kid. Shes been missing for hours and there are search teams from Canada and the US looking for her.

Thats terrible! says Katy. She must be scared to death.

Her parents were picked up by American customs trying to walk across the river.

Really. Crossing the river eh? says Katy. She looks back at me.

The parents are on there way here says the sarjent. We are the nearest police station. Everyone's panicking of course—Adeline is still missing. There are police and CBSA teams looking for her on this side of the river and home land security has people on the other side.

One of the sarjents phones rings. She says yes and then okay.

The baby is looking all over the place. Sharp eyes she has.

Ad she says. Ad ad ad.

Or is it dad dad dad?

Im not your dad I tell her.

Im not worryed about her like I was when she was cold. But theres something. It has to do with us being in the police station and her calling me dad. In a few minits I will hand her over and the police will take care of her. She wont be my baby any more.

Katy is talking to the sarjent about the missing kid. She must be safe now Katy says. Its so cold. Shes probly in a coffee shop.

You dont understand says the sarjent. Adeline is a baby.

What? says Katy. I thot you were talking about a teenager.

Not even a year old says the sarjent. The parents were carrying 2 bags—1 with close and an other with the baby in it. When the chase started they hid 1 bag to move faster. They thot it was the bag of close but it turned out to be Adeline.

Ad says the baby on my lap.

And then the door opens and a rush of cold air comes into the police station. I hear shouting and crying and muttering. 3 people rush down the hall past me and up to the desk. The woman is shouting and the man is crying and the customs officer is muttering.

Find her! shouts the woman. Find her!

She is wearing a green parka and has dark hair and big eyes. She looks like a bomb has gone off inside her.

The man has his hands in front of his face. Hes crying. The customs officer holds the neck of his coat practicly carrying him along—witch she can do easily. Thats how big she is.

Im watching you she mutters.

Shut up! says the woman. Your people havent found her.

Were looking says the officer. Now that your back in Canada where you belong your baby is our number 1 priority. We all want the same thing she says.

This happens in a few seconds while they are walking in front of us. The baby tries to jump out of my lap and I have to hold on tite. Her mouth opens.

Mama! Mama!

The woman is at my side so fast I do not see her move. It is like magic—she is yelling at the customs officer and then she is holding the baby. I culd not stop her if I wanted to. She wants the baby more than I have ever wanted anything.

Adeline she says. Adeline. Adeline.

She is crying but not boo hoo. Tears pour down her cheeks like rain. Like a waterfall. I have never seen crying like that befor.

Mama! says the baby. Mama!

The 2 of them are holding each other so tite I can not tell where mom stops and baby starts. It is like they are 1 person—like mom is pregnant again.

There is a thump. The man has fallen to the floor.

The customs officer is not enjoying the family reunion. Shes staring at me.

You! she says.

She is Brady or Alex—I dont know witch. The bigger tuffer 1.

Your in trouble she says. Theres a red file on you. You belong in America.

No I say. I want to stay here.

She lifts Adelines dad up by his coat and drops him in the corner.

These folks will have to stay she says. But we will see about you.

Then she goes over to talk to the sarjent. I dont know why she has it so upside down. Why cant she take Adelines family back with her and leave me here? Then we wuld all be happy.

Katy comes over to sit beside me. Shes got a big smile on her face. She nods at Adeline and her mom who are still hugging each other. They havent moved.

See what you did? she says.

HOURS LATER IT IS SO LATE IT IS EARLY.

Katys on a new pack of smokes. Ive told my story to Brady or Alex and 2 customs officers from Canada and Ive answered questions—lots of them. Im real tired.

Adelines gone. Her and her family mite stay in Canada and mite have to go someplace far away—to make it harder to sneek into America next time. Sounds pretty stupid to me but maybe I have it wrong. I got to hold Adeline 1 more time to say goodbye. Not that I care. Shes just a baby. Her mom has finally stopped crying.

Brady or Alex is gone 2 and I did not go with her no matter how much she talked about hot per suit.

Let me tell you about hot per suit. That is a big deal. Brady or Alex said she culd take me back across the border because she grabbed me in America and I ran away so when she saw me here it was hot per suit and hot per suit gave her special powers. The Canadian customs officers said hot per suit was no good in my case. Yes it is said Brady or Alex. No it isnt said the Canadian customs guys. Yes it is. No it isnt. What about home land security? said Brady or Alex. That doesnt matter said the Canadian guys. Yes it does. No it doesnt.

I may be wrong about some of this but trust me—hot per suit is important. They must of said it 1000 times. The police sarjent was with them on this. She nodded her head every time.

Katy solved the problem by saying she drove me here because I wanted to come and that wasnt hot per suit or cold per suit or any other kind of per suit and anyway I saved the babys life so go home you bully. Thats what she called Brady or Alex. A bully.

Brady or Alex put on her coat and hat and stomped over to where I was sitting. She leaned down—close enuff for me to smell her gum. Peppermint.

I still dont trust you she told me. You could be a terrorist.

A terrorist? said the young Canadian customs officer—the 1 who looks like Superman. Thats ridiculous! he said.

Katy laffed. Brady or Alex left the station. Her uniform boots made for good stomping. I never did find out her name.

That was a bit ago. Now its so late its early. Im not going back to America tonite but I am still in trouble. The older Canadian customs officer wants me to show Im a citizen even tho I dont have a pass port.

In case the Americans come back with proofs of there own he says. I have some questions for you— Canadian questions. Theyll only take a minit. You can answer them eh?

Hes got white hair and a great voice. If the other officer is Superman this 1 is like that guy who plays God in the movies.

Uhh I say.

Lets begin with an easy 1. Do you know whos the prime minister? he asks me.

No. Oh no wait. That guy I say. With the glasses and the funny hair. I saw him shaking hands with Aiden Tween on TV.

Katys back from a smoke. She hears this and laffs. She thinks Im pretty funny.

Sorry I say to the old officer.

Well do you know any capitals? he asks me.

Washington DC I say rite away. And Beijing.

I can even spell it. I did a project on Beijing for school because Mr Wing is from there. The old guy frowns at me.

No he says.

What—they changed it? I say.

I mean our capitals he says.

Hes shorter than the Superman guy but hes the boss. His uniform has things on the sholders to show hes important.

Oh yeah. Sorry I say. I remember now. Ottawa is our capital. Mom goes there sometimes. Its in Ontario I say.

Any more?

We have *more* capitals?

He looks out the window.

I know eh? I say. Sorry Im so stupid.

Im afraid hes going to send me to America for not knowing stuff so I try to come up with Canadian things. I think hard.

I know Terry Fox I say. And Wayne Gretzky. And that singer—whats her name. The one who sings about the river she can skate away on. Theyre Canadian rite? And Aiden Tween but I gess every bodys herd of him. And that singer from Montreal. And the basketball player that Benj likes. And those guys who discovered gravity—no not gravity but something important. Insulation. Something like that. Some doctor thing. There Canadian. I know they are I say.

The customs boss shakes his head and lets out a long haaaaa. Not a laff. He looks more like that God actor than ever.

You shuld go home now sir says the younger officer. I can take care of Bunny here.

I feel horrible. I failed the test.

I am Canadian I call after him. Sorry but I really am.

I turn to the younger guy with the muscles and chin and the lick of hair curling over his fore head.

Dont drive me back to America I beg him.

Katy puts her hand on my arm.

Its okay Bunny she says. He believes your Canadian. His boss beleeves you. Everybody beleeves you.

But I got the questions wrong I say.

Yeah she says. Yeah you did. But its the way you did.

She heads for home. On her way out the door she yawns and shoots me with her finger. Shes pretty cool.

The Superman customs officer is going to look after me.

HIS NAME IS BROZ.

He says I can call him Joe. He sits beside me and gets out a tape recorder. He puts in a what do you call it—a cart ridge—and presses a button to turn it on.

This is customs officer Joseph Broz at 6 AM on Dec 31st he says.

He points the recorder at me and tells me to introduce myself and xplain what is going on and how I came here.

You want to know everything? I say.

Yes.

But—everything?

And speak slowly.

So I do.

My name is Bunny I say into the recorder. I am 15 and a bit—almost 16. I live at Creekside Juvenile Detention Centre. I dont know the address but it is near the train tracks in Hope Springs. That is in Ontario in Canada. I am out on a pass. My PO gave it to me. Her name is Roz. I came home for Christmas and then we drove up to my grampas cottage. I was with my brother and my cousins. My brothers name is Spencer.

I take a breath and try to think about what happened and when.

It is way easier to tell a story than it is to write it down. Last time I had to write down a story it took all day. This story only takes a little while. The police station gets noisy as cops come in and the day starts. It is still dark outside. I keep talking.

Joe is interested. He wants to know about the kid nappers. What are there names? Where are they from? What do they want? I tell him Vi and Lubor and Peter and Bojan. And the anthem. And Dusan I say but I never saw him.

Joe stops the tape.

Did your grandfather spend time in—some place? he asks. I do not recognize the name. The way he says it there is a lot of spitting in it.

I dont know I say. Is that a country?

It is now says Joe. But it wasnt when your grampa was spying. Thats what he was rite? A spy?

I gess so I say. There were pass ports and money in his wall. Those are spy things and he was hiding them. And we found a gun. My cousins think he was a spy and there pretty smart. Spencers smart for sure.

And he got the anthem says Joe. Rite? Isnt that what the SPCA kid nappers want?

I dont even know there name. SPCA—what is that? You know more than me I say.

Joes face changes. Oh he says. I thot you said the name.

No. I never herd of the SPCA.

I gess I got it wrong says Joe.

He starts the tape again. You keep talking he tells me. Finish your story while I make some phone calls.

A gust of warm air blows up from the floor. Im so tired. I culd sleep until spring. I close my eyes and feel my body melting like butter on the stove.

I do not dream.

Floating away from a street full of zombies in my new iron hat to play moon tag with my friend Akie from grade 2 until my mom calls to ask what I want on my cheese burger—*thats* a dream. Crazy you know? I had that exact dream last month.

So what I have now is not a dream. Its like I am sleeping and awake at the same time. I know I am in a police station in skates that pinch a bit and close that smell pretty bad. I have my head down and my eyes closed. And I hear Grampas voice. Careful Bernard he says.

It takes me back to the time we were walking near the cottage and I went after a snake that didnt run away. Well not run—it was a snake so it culdnt run. But it didnt slide away. What it did was it looped around on itself and waited. This was years ago when I was like 8 or 10. It was just me and Grampa.

He pulled me away from the snake and said Careful Bernard. Then he showed me the rattles on the snakes tail and told me what they meant and we walked on.

Careful Bernard. Thats what I hear now. I wake up from my not dream with Grampas voice in my ears.

GOOD NEWS.

Joe is taking the day off work so he can drive me to Creekside.

Its not far to Creekside he says. If we leave now youll be there this afternoon.

I make sure and thank him. He says no problem. Standing up we are the same size witch means he is a skate taller than me.

Joe drives a police car xept it does not have flashing lites or a siren and it is green. Joe is like a cop under cover—but not very far under cover. I sit in the big front seat. The sun shines in my face. There is a sheepskin rug on the drivers seat but not on mine so Joe can be warm and comfy but not me. Oh well. On the dash in front of me is a sticker of a flag I do not know.

Joe skids a bit coming out of the parking lot. It is still icy.

The clock says 7:34. Spencer will be awake. I ask Joe if I can use his cell phone to call my brother. He says no.

My phone battery is dead he says. Sorry Bunny.

We slip and slide getting onto the 401 but the hi way is clear and we go fast. Trees and fields flash past us and the tires hum and every time I look up there is another turnoff. I am thinking about how nice it will be to eat and sleep and not worry when I get back to Creekside. Especially not worry.

Worrying is hard on you. Its a voice thats always there. Worry worry worry worry worry worry worry worry. You dont notice it and dont notice it and dont notice it and then you do—and you realize its been there all along. Ive been worrying ever since they grabbed me from the city hall rink. Finally I dont have to worry. Im in an almost police car on my way home. I try to shake off the voice. Worry worry worry worry.

There are snowy fields on both sides of the hi way with trees behind them. White and dark with the blu sky on top. I take a deep breath.

The clock says *10:04*.

Whats that? I ask Joe. Pointing at the sticker on the dash.

Oh that is the coat of arms of—some place he says.

If I was going to try to spell the some place it would come out Pee Yan Vee Ah. Thats not the way Joe says it but I cant write down his spitting and clearing his throat sounds.

I try to say it. Pee Yan Vee Yah?

I know that name. Ive herd it befor.

Close says Joe.

The sun glints off his teeth for a second when he smiles. He really does look like Superman—or maybe an ad for beer or happyness.

We pass a truck and a small car.

Wait—isnt Pee Yan Vee Yah the place you asked about back at the police station? I say. You wanted to know if my grampa had been there.

I was interested he says. My mother and father were born there. Im Canadian but my background is

Pee Yan Vee Yan. Theres a lot of us in Canada he says. Toronto and Montreal have big Pee Yan Vee Yan communities. And Winnipeg.

Sure I say.

The next sine is for a gas station. Joe puts on his turn signal. Were running low he says. And Im hungry. Do you want a sandwich?

Sure I say.

There are 4 gas tanks under a tall roof. Joe gets out and rolls his sholders to make them looser. I stay in and yawn. When I stretch my left hand touches the rug on Joe's seat. Its fur not sheepskin. Huh.

The country side is bumpy like the blankets when you get out of bed. The sun is above the trees. Its a winter sun—more white than yellow. Its trying to warm you up but it cant.

Joe goes into the Tim Hortons next door. He has his phone up to his ear and he is shaking his head. I check the driver rug. It is fur all rite—an entire animal. The hind legs hang down in front and the head stretches over the back of the seat under the head rest.

A wolf.

WEIRD EH?

All the wolf stuff. I can hear the worry voice in my head. No reason for this since my adventure is over and I am on my way home. But I dont like the idea of killing a wolf and skinning him and sitting on him. Whether hes your grampa or not doesnt matter. Its not cool. And thats not the only thing. Joe was lying about his phone. He said it wasnt working and it is. Is there anything else hes lying about?

Worry worry worry worry worry.

Joe drives away with a jerk and eats his sandwich in chomps. His cheeks are smoother than Dads. They move all the time—even after he finishes eating.

He taps the steering wheel. Dad would tell him to chill. He says that to Mom a lot. It is his way of saying to take it easy.

We pass a sine that says *TORONTO* 113.

Do you know the way to Creekside? Joe asks me.

No I say. Sorry.

My sandwich is meat and cheese like Joes. And mustard. Its pretty good.

But do you know where it is?

Not really.

He nods like he is pleased.

No problem he says. I do. You relax for a while.

Joe is driving me and getting me lunch but he wont let me use his phone. So he is being nice to me but he is also not being nice to me. That doesnt make sense. Something else is going on.

I finish my sandwich and milk. The numbers on the sines get smaller and smaller. *Toronto* 78. *Toronto* 56. Joe doesnt talk and nether do I. I close my eyes. I feel like I am waiting for a balloon to pop. Something is about to happen. I know it. I just *know* it.

Worry worry worry worry worry.

I open my eyes. Close them. Open them again. Nothing happens. We keep driving.

So much for what I know.

The road gets wider. 3 lanes then 4 then a hole bunch. Ive been here befor. We pass a mall with a gas station and a dollar store and a Happy New Year banner. The road bends and the land falls away so I get a wide view of the lake on my left. It goes all the way to the horizon and there is ice a long way out. The sun bounces off it. The clock ticks from 12:23 to 12:24. Theres lots of cars on the road and they are going fast.

Joe puts on his turn signal and swoops over. We are off the 401 but where are we?

Is this how you get to Creekside? I ask.

It isnt how the bus took me there from the court house in Toronto. And its not how mom and dad took me home last week.

Joes hair shines with whatever he puts in it.

We are going to stop for a moment on our way to Creekside he says. I have to drop something off.

Oh I say.

We turn and turn again and drive down a twisty street. We are in the middle of a lot of houses and all of them look the same. Same front window and porch. Same roof with 2 pointy bits facing the street. Same little tree on the front lawn—maybe even the same kind of tree. Same drive way with the snow cleared away and piled up. Same garage with the house number on the front. Different numbers.

We come to a stop sine but dont stop. The car going the other way honks at us. We roll slowly down the street while Joe reads the numbers.

We stop in front of the only house on the street with the drive way full of snow.

This is the place says Joe.

He zooms the engine. We skid sideways up the curb and bucket forward up the drive way and then stop.

Come inside Bunny.

Joes voice is harsher than normal. It is stretched like he is. Everything about him is tite like plastic rap on a bowl.

Just for a bit he says.

I dont want to come inside but I have to go to the bathroom so I unbuckle my seat belt and open the car door. Joe puts his hand on my sholder and steers me up the front steps. There is a front door key in the male box.

The place smells like sickness. You know what I mean. Spencers bedroom smells like that when he has the flu. I dont know what makes the smell. Barf and swet I gess. Sheets and dirty close and pills—no maybe not pills. I take off my skates and think yuck. Its worse down the hall in the bathroom but I have to go so I try not to notice it. I do notice Grampas voice tho—it cuts thru the toilet flushing and me washing my hands.

Bernard you must hurry.

I jump enuff to splash water on my pants and socks.

Grampa? I wisper.

I cant see where he is. The meer reflects the hole bathroom but Im the only 1 there.

I turn off the water and dry my hands—and spot the geography magazine on the shelf behind the towels. I havent been to the dentist in a while so I havent seen this one. The front cover has a close up of a wolf staring into the camera. Big yellow eyes serious and sad. The headline reads *WILD BUT NOT CRAZY*.

That would be Grampa.

WE HAVE A BATHROOM CONVERSATION

—me and the wolf on the cover of the magazine. The toilet runs for a bit and the fan is on so nobody can hear us.

This house is dangerous for you Bernard.

Why? I ask.

The wolfs eyes gleam like they are alive when Grampa is speaking. Then they go back to paper. Gleam and fade—gleam and fade. They gleam now.

Broz is 1 of them says the wolf.

One of—

The Pee Yan Vee Yan national party he says.

He spits the name like Joe does. And like an old movy clip coming back I remember the hockey game I played back at the Newman house. A mask guy told me he was from a place that sounded like a Pee and a Vee—and so was a player for the Vancouver hockey team. I didnt know if Pee and Vee was a city or a country or what. Now I realize he was talking about Pee Yan Vee Yah. And that the Pee Yan Vee Yah guys are the kid nappers.

Lots of people are from there I say to Grampa. Just because your from Pee Yan Vee Yah doesnt mean your a kid napper. Joe is a customs officer I say.

And a lyer. He never called Creekside about you Bernard. He drove past the turnoff to get here.

Worry worry worry worry worry worry worry worry worry worry.

He lyed about his phone 2 I say.

The kid nappers needed a safe place to drive you across the border says Grampa. They new where Joe works. They are a nationalist group called the SPCA.

That was the name Joe asked me about!

Hush Bernard! Speak more quietly.

Sorry I wisper.

I know the wolf stuff doesnt makes sense. I get that. *Its about how much you trust Grampa.* Spencer was talking about spying and who Grampa was working for. But I dont care about that. He led me to Adeline. Saving her life is the biggest and best thing Ive done in a long time. Maybe ever. Babys are more important than spy secrets. Take that James Bond. Id rather have Grampa on my side.

What shuld I do now? I ask him.

Theres a window behind you. Use it.

What?

You promised you would look after yourself Bernard. Keep your promise.

The cover wolf uses a very Grampa tone of voice. The yellow eyes blaze like fire and then the lite in them goes out. The magazine is just a magazine.

There is a name on it. The magazine is delivered to Violet Dieters. Whoever that is. This must be her house. The address is in Toronto.

Holy crap! Grampa was rite—Im way past Creekside.

I stare at myself in the meer for a second. A big rumply boy with dark hair sticking out and a look of Holy crap! on his face. That's me all rite.

I have to stand on the toilet to reach the window. It is small but I can push myself thru the open part even in my coat witch I am still wearing. I am worryed about my feet. I will run faster in socks than in skates—but not for long.

You probly think I am crazy. Fair enuff. It doesnt make sense that Grampa is helping me from beyond the grave—but sense isnt everything. It doesnt make sense that I found a baby in a gym bag. It doesnt make sense that Aiden Tween is so popular. It doesnt make sense that people smoke cigarets or feed stray cats or kill children or like pickle flavor potato chips—but they do. It doesnt make sense that you are reading this story insted of all the other millions of stories out there. Life isnt about making sense. Its a gift and you do your best with it. Yeah its crazy that Grampa is talking to me but it would also be crazy for me not to pay attention—like saying no to the gift. If you need help and you get help you shuld use the help.

IT IS AN EASY DROP FROM THE BATHROOM WINDOW

to the ground and I am out and running. The back yard is covered in a clean sheet of snow. My footprints are huge—a giant smashing his way across the earth. Joe will have no problem following me. I hop over the back fence and keep running. The snow is up to my knees. I run thru to the street. Now the snow is smashed down and you can not tell where Ive been.

I run up the drive way of the first house and pound on the door.

Help! I shout.

The porch lite comes on and I hear noises behind the door. Somebody is there. But they are not opening the door. What they are doing is watching me thru the peep hole.

Its OK! I shout. I am not dangerous!

Mind you I am hopping because my feet are cold. I must look weerd. I try again.

I am not crazy! I shout. Let me in! The Pee Yan Vee Yans are after me!

That sounds pretty crazy tho doesnt it.

No wait they really are! Help! Please let me in!

Nothing. I will have to think of better stuff to yell. No more Pee Yan Vee Yans. Nobody is home at the next house or the 1 after. The house after that has lots of lites up and a mess on the front porch—a broken sled and a mitt and a hat that a kid has dropped. A mom comes to the door when I ring the bell but she will not let me in.

Go away! she says. Please go away!

The door is on a chain lock. I can see a strip of her face. She is scared of me—a crazy stranger.

Im cold! I shout. I have no shoes!

Her face softens. I can feel her weaken. She is a mom after all.

Please let me in! I shout. I have to get back to jail!

The door slams. Drat.

I am so mad I kick the kids hat off the porch—
and find a cell phone lying underneath! Wuld you
believe it? It must have fallen out of the moms
pocket befor the kid started losing his close. Its the
same kind as my phone. I push the start button to
turn it on.

My hart has been on a trampoline trip for the last
few minits. Good luck bad luck good luck. Up down
up. I escape from Joe—up!—but my feet are freezing—
down!—but heres a house with people—up!—but they
wont take me in—down!—but heres a cell phone—up!
But it doesnt work. I cant turn on the darn thing. I gess
theres no power.

Down.

I hold out the phone so the mom can see it and
ring the bell again. Let me in and I will give it to you!
I shout.

Wait—that sounds nasty.

Your phone I mean!

Nothing.

I slip the broken phone in my pocket and start
running. No sidewalks so I head down the middle of
the road. My breath steams in the street lites. I try not
to think about my feet. I cant. Joe will be looking for

me so I have to hurry. I wish I had my skates. I can go faster on skates and they keep my feet warmer.

I come to a stop sine with a line of 3 or 4 cars. I cant see the people in the cars but they can see me. I stick out my thum like I want to hitch hike. Nothing happens for a second and then 1 of the cars ahead of me honks. The back door opens. I hurry over and slide into the warm.

Thank you I say to guy in the back seat. He has a scarf over his face. His eyes are wide like he is surprised. Thank you thank you.

I am bouncing high on the trampoline of good luck.

I bend over and rub my feet thru my socks. Oh. Oh. Oh that feels good.

The car takes off and makes a turn. And another. I sit up. My name is Bunny I say. Please take me out of here. I need to find a phone. I am going to—

And then I fall rite off the luck trampoline and land with a thud.

O crap I say.

The guy beside me takes off his scarf. His hair is pointy at the front. Its Lubor. Vi is in the front passenger seat. I do not know the driver but he is smiling into the meer and not in a nice way. I am back with the kid nappers.

When I try to scramble out of the car Lubor grabs me pretty hard.

No he says.

With Lubors axent it doesnt sound like the way I say no but thats what he means.

VI TURNS AROUND.

The lites from the street and the houses shine off her face. Shes still nice looking. I want to hate her but I cant. Is it because she is pretty? Yes. Yes it is.

Do you know how long we have been following you? she asks me. All the way from Perivale.

I dont know the name. Oh wait—I remember now.

Steves place I say.

That idiot! says Vi. I don't know how Lubors mom can work for him. And then to the border and all the way to Toronto. We kept just missing you!

You were in the US customs shed just ahead of us and then you escaped. Youve been lucky all day long.

Lucky? And here I am thinking about my unluck. But I gess Ive been lucky 2. Maybe everybody is lucky and unlucky—it depends on who is looking.

Vi leans back over the seat and slaps me across the face. It hurts.

Thats for the flat tires she says.

Maybe I dont like her so much even tho she is pretty.

We turn a corner and another and pull up outside the place I ran away from. Joe is outside looking grim. He gets happier when he sees me get out of the car with Lubors hand on my arm. We all go inside the house.

Joe holds the door open for the driver and then for Vi. Lubor and I go in on our own. Joe and Lubor talk for a while in back-of-the-throat language. I know what they are saying even if I do not know the words. Lubor is mad and Joe is trying to xplain.

They throw me in a basement room and lock the door.

SO AFTER ALL MY SKATING AND RUNNING AND HIDING

I am kid napped again. The room is white and cold and empty xept for a clock on the wall. Thats all there is in the room—a big round 6:01. I have no idea what they use this room for—telling time is all you can do. Now its 6:03. I sit down on the cement floor. After a while my bottom feels cold so I stand up. 6:14. Now my feet feel cold.

I feel I shuld do something. Anything. Waiting for your luck to change is not enuff. Good luck happens when you do something. And if it doesnt happen at least you feel better. 6:16. I throw my sholder against the door. It does not move.

I try again—harder. Nope. I try kicking the door. Nothing happens and now my sock foot and my sholder are both sore. Doing something doesnt always make you feel better. 6:19.

I take the phone I found on the ladys porch out of my coat pocket. It is still not working. I put it in my pants pocket.

At 6:20 the door opens and Joe walks in with the driver who is smaller and thinner than Joe but more important. Joe stands back and lets him talk.

So here you are in Toronto Bunny he says. You traveled a long way and nearly escaped but we have you now. It is a long journey for my country also— my poor suffering Pee Yan Vee Yah! And tonite the journey ends he says. Your grampa stole our anthem. Your brother found it. Tonite the world will hear it— and they will weep!

I gess the anthem is sad. I never cry during our anthem. We stand on gard for the—so what? Also we sing it about 80 times. I want to shout We know! Were going to stand on gard! We get it.

Not gard—something else. Gaurd maybe or guard—but that just looks wrong. Yes wrong. English is harder than it has to be. The driver has a wispy

beerd and long hair and talks like Lubor only more
so. He reminds me of somebody.

You must phone him he says to me.

Phone—

Your brother. Tell him you are in our power and
he must do what we want. You will do it now.

The driver punches a number on his sell phone
and hands it to me. I finally realize what is going on—
what has been going on all along. These guys from
Pee Yan Vee Yah are kid napping me so that Spencer
will do something for them!

What do you want my brother to do? I ask. The
phone is ringing in my ear.

He knows what to do says the driver. Talk to him.
Let him hear your voice.

Who does the driver remind me of?

The phone rings a bit more and then stops.

Sorry I say. I cant get thru.

We try again and again and then the driver gives
up and turns to go. On his way out he pats Joe on the
back—witch he has to reach up to do.

You keep trying Joe he says. You and Lubor and Vi
are in charge of Bunny. Get him to talk to his brother.

I am going to the square now to check on the others. Keep Bunny safe for now he says.

For now? I think. What does that mean—for now?

We all look at the clock. 6:32.

Sure Dusan says Joe.

Dusan?

I know the name now—I thot it was Susan the first time I herd it.

Your Dusan? I say to the driver.

He is standing in the door way.

It is 1 of my names he says and walks away.

He knows what he wants. And hes neat and tidy—even tho he has a lame mustash. If I ever see Dusan again I will tell him who he reminds me of. Hell be surprised.

Joe walks out with him. The door slams shut. Its just me and the clock now.

6:35.

I think about Spencer doing something to save me because I am kid napped. I do not like the thot at all. I wonder wuld I do something to save him? Course I wuld. But I am unhappy. It is no fun to need saving.

I wish I was back in the police station. Then I culd call Spencer and tell him I am safe and he wuld not have to do the thing that Dusan wants him to do. Even Bets jail is better than here. I worked hard and came a long way to be here like Dusan said—but I ended up in the worst place I can be.

I feel bad and useless and a failure and my feet hurt. I wonder what I can do. Words come back to me. Do what you say your going to do. Help as many as you can. These are good things to have on your grave stone. He helped many. He did what he said he would. But I still feel bad. 6:36.

Im yawning all the time.

The wolfs words come back to me—take care of yourself Bernard.

Im not mad at him—the wolf I mean. Im not mad at Grampa ether. I culd be mad because he didnt tell me Vi and Dusan were in the car. But I still trust him and I will try to take care of myself. The clock says 6:38.

When I wake up it says 11:15. I do some push ups and some jumps. Sleep helped me. I'm ready to go. Thanks for the advice Grampa. I feel better. Witch is funny because talking to Grampa didn't always make me feel better when he was alive.

WE TRY DIFFERENT PHONES.

Lubors and Vis and Joes. I remember how Joe told me his phone didnt work. Now he wants me to use it and it really doesnt work. What do they call that kind of joke? Its not funny. But something.

11:35.

If I was back at Creekside it would be lites out.

You didnt call Creekside did you? I ask Joe. But hes not paying attention. He frowns at the phone in my hand witch rings and then stops. We are not getting thru. I remember the old lady who thot I was God. *Not even you can get the phones to work* she said. Joe presses redial and we try again. Still nothing.

Why doesnt Vis mom have a landline? he mutters.

I know a bit about what is going on by now. Theres a New Years Eve concert and something is going to happen and it will be about Pee Yan Vee Yah. Thats all I know for sure because Lubor and Joe talk a lot of Pee Yan Vee Yan and I have no idea what there saying. And even when they speak English I do not know what they mean a lot of the time. They talk about 80 a lot. Is 80 there yet? Whos with 80? When is 80 going on? Will 80 know the words?

What is this 80? I asked when I was trying Vis phone.

It was like 80 was somebodys uncle—or an animal like a hamster.

80 is old if its a person I said.

And if theres an 80 year old hamster its a miracle.

80 is letters Vi told me. A and T.

Oh. AT. Whoever that is.

Her phone didnt work either.

That was a few minits ago. Now it is 11:47 and they are all back in the room together and something is going on because they have coats and boots on. Joe holds my skates.

We have to get closer he says. AT will be going onstage soon and we have to find a phone signal. Come on.

We walk upstares. Joe and Lubor hold onto my arms. Vi talks to me.

We are going for a car ride she says. Its about twenty minits from here to the concert. We need you to be awake to talk to your brother. So you have to be good. No running away. No shouting ok?

I dont know what to say. There are more of them and they are bigger and stronger than me and I have no shoes.

Promise? she says. Promise you will not try to escape and you can sit in the car until we find a signal from your brothers phone.

I shake my head.

I cant promise I say.

Im wondering if she will slap me again but she doesnt.

Lubor! she calls.

Next thing I know there is a thing on my head like a blanket or something. I cant see. Lubor and I gess Joe grab my arms and legs and carry me outside.

Help! I yell. Help!!

Nobody comes to save me. Im thrown into a place that smells like dust. I hear a click and then silence. It takes me a while to get free of the blanket because I cant see or stretch out very far. When my head is clear I still cant see. Its super dark. There are 2 lumps near me—my skates. And a bigger lump under me—a spare tire. I hear a familiar rumbling noise and feel a vibration around but mostly under me. We start to move.

BUMP BUMP SLIDE BUMP.

Ow. I am an idiot. Why didnt I promise not to escape? I could be sitting in the back seat of the car rite now insted of sliding around the trunk getting hurt every time we run over a pot hole or stop at a stop sine.

Bump bump bump. This is how it all started—me in the trunk. I dont know how much time I will have befor they get a phone signal. I shuld get ready to escape. The only thing I can think of is to put on my skates. Its not much of an idea but a skater can move quick across the ice. If theres ice.

I twist around like a worm on a fish hook to get my skates on my sore feet. It takes a while in the dark with all the bumps and jolts. I work up a swet. I am the hottest I have been since I dont know when. But at last the skates are on. I take a breath. If theres ice on the Toronto streets I can maybe get away.

The pop song surprises me. Not witch song it is— You baby you baby you are the 1. You hear that song all the time. Aiden Tween is hard to miss. But I dont expect to hear him coming out of my pants.

I reach into my pocket and pull out the phone. Its working now. Full power. There were no bars befor but now they are all lit up. Lites are flashing.

Befor I can say hello into the phone I hear a loud voice tell me Ive won a chance to go on a dream vacation. Lucky you! says the voice. Its a what do you call them—guys who sell stuff on the phone. Only its really a tape recording. Mom hates them. She shouts into the phone until Dad tells her to chill. Then she slams down the phone and shouts at Dad.

I end the call and stare at the phone. This is my chance. I dont know why the phone is working but it is. I slide up my coat sleeve and my shirt sleeve and use the lite from the phone to read the number on my arm. The call to my brother goes thru—first time tonite. I am about to give up when the ringing stops and Spencer says hi. I say hi.

BUNNY! HE SAYS.

He recognizes my voice rite away and he sounds really happy to hear from me. I almost start to cry. I dont tho. He asks where I am.

In Toronto I say. In a car.

Fantastic Bun! he shouts. Your home safe.

Well actually—I start but he interrupts me.

Mom said you would be okay he says. Man am I ever glad.

Mom? I say.

Yeah. She knows all about you. She sees this you know.

At least thats what I think he says. I dont understand. What can Mom see? Doesnt matter—I dont have much time. If the signal is good enough to get thru now then Joe will be stopping the car soon.

Spencer call the cops I say. Tell them—

And I stop. Its my usual problem. I dont know enuff. I dont know whats going on at the concert or where Dusan is or the license plate of this car. I dont even know anything about AT xept its probly not a hamster. But I have a working phone and a chance to talk to my brother. This is help and I shuld use it.

Im going to get away Spencer I say. I have my skates. So dont do it ok?

Dont—

Whatever they want you to do at the concert I say. Dusan and those guys. The kid nappers. Dont do it.

I cant hear you Bun he says.

And dont worry about me.

Dont—

Dont worry! I almost shout.

OK see you soon he says. Have fun.

He clicks off.

Fun? What does he think is going on? Has he herd anything I said?

I didnt get a chance to tell him about Dusan. Theres a mistery—or why would Dusan remind me of Jade? Im sure theres a reason. Jade is a mistery 2. But Spencer hung up so quick I didnt get a chance to say any of this.

Bump. Bump. It feels like the car is running over a bunch of holes. Bump bump bump.

And then the world ends with a—

BANG!

Thats what it sounds like.

BANG!

Something is happening in front of me. Something loud—like firecrackers or bombs. The car starts to spin. 1 time around. 2 times. Are the bombs part of the Pee Yan Vee Yah plan? There is a down and an up as well as a round and round. I feel like I am on a ride at Wonderland only I cant see anything and I dont have a seat belt on. I keep bumping into parts of the trunk.

BANG!

Another loud something happens beside me and we start spinning the other way. Noises are coming from all over. Horns and brake squeals and yells. Loud yells. Weird ones that dont even sound human. Whatevers going on is big and bad and lasts a long time. If this was a TV show itd be in slow motion. And its all in the dark.

I remember the word I was trying to think of befor. Telemarketer. Thats the word.

Time keeps going by.

The car stops spinning. Im pressed against the side of the trunk. The car is tilted with my side lower than the other. I wait. I have no idea what to expect. Its still noisy outside—like Im inside a thunderstorm. And then comes the loudest thunder clap of all—the one where the storm is rite over head and the thunder and the litening come together.

CRACK!!

It happens rite at my feet. I shoot forward and hit my sholder on something. The trunk pops wide open. Its cold. I take a breath and shake my head to clear it. Im looking up. I can see a moon and some street lites and the front of a station wagon that bumped into us from behind and popped the trunk.

Do something.

I have to do something.

My brain is slow—I mean its always slow but it is even slower now. I hear a scream. And another. And then a lot of bellowing.

Do something.

Escape! Rite. This is my chance. I sit up and the world spins. I have to shake my head again. Come on Bunny.

I start to crawl out. I have my hand on the edge of the trunk when I take a look around and realize how very strange the hole thing is.

I KNOW SOME OF THE TRUTH RITE AWAY.

I find some out later. And some of it I still dont know. Heres what I see from the trunk of Joes car.

We are in a field of ice and snow. Not a farm field—a city kind. We are in Toronto. The white gates of the CNE are rite over there. I can see them. Theres a road on my left and then an other field with a baseball diamond and then Lake Ontario witch is big and dark and empty. On my rite is a street going up a hill and a big overpass. The grounds uneven and thats why we are tilted. The station wagon that popped the trunk is near by. It bounced back and there is a big white balloon in the front seat. All around me are cows.

Yes thats what I said.

The biggest thing in the field is a huge truck that carries cows. Used to I mean. You know the kind of truck—it has holes in the sides for the cows to breath. Or the pigs or whatever animal. This truck was carrying cows and now it is lying half on its side in the middle of the field with the back doors open. The cows are out. Some of them are rite there. I dont think Ive ever been this close to cows befor. You know what—they are big. These are anyway. They are black and white and as tall as the car. They have horns and round wet eyes. There breath comes out in clouds around there heads.

Im surprised by the axident—the bangs and the spinning around—and Im surprised to find myself in a place I know like the CNE but I am even more surprised by the cows. I dont know what I expect when the trunk pops up but not this. I find out later that the cow truck hit a patch of ice and skidded across 2 lanes and into the icy field. Our car and the station wagon were beside the truck and it carried us along. Nobody was hurt in the crash itself—all the injuries happen now.

Joe and Vi and Lubor are all ready out of the car. They see me. Lubor moves toward the trunk. He has a phone in his hand and a grim nasty look on his face.

Wheres AT now? he says into the phone.

Do something I think. I will have to be fast if I want to get away.

Watch out! yells Joe. These cows are spooked.

What do you mean? says Lubor. They are just cows.

No no says Joe. I live in the country and I have seen—

Lubor tries to push a cow out of the way. Something happens that I can not see and he goes down screaming. Vi drops to her nees to help him and the cow kicks her. I see this. Vi is beside the cow and the animal lifts its leg side ways and kicks Vi in the neck. Really—a side ways kick. Vi goes sprawly on the ice beside Lubor whose leg is bent in a way that makes me sick to look at. The cow lifts her head and bellows loud and long. Its a cow noise but it sounds like a truck going up hill. She starts to run. The other cows follow her—big and slippy sloppy and crazy mad.

I watch Vi because I want to know if she is alive. She is. She moves her head and then puts it back down on the ice again.

The cows slide around the field like birds flying this way and then that way.

The driver of the station wagon is a man in a suit and tie and nice coat and gloves. He looks like hes just come from the bank. When he sees the cows he climbs back inside the car with the big white balloon in the front seat.

Do something.

I step down from the trunk onto the ice and take a wobbly stride on my skates—and theres Joe with his super strong hand on my arm. He's got me again. I try to pull away but Joe hangs on.

I am not letting you go he says.

Why?

He doesnt anser.

Why? I say louder.

Im not asking about letting go. I want to know why they are doing this. Why kid nap me and chase me around? What does it matter about where Grampa put the anthem? What does it matter if Spencer finds it? Whats it all about?

Joe understands. He nods.

I love my country he says.

What? Canada?

He shakes his head.

Pee Yan Vee Yah is my real home country he

says—and it is not free. I would do anything to free it. Lubor and Vi feel the same way. And Dusan. We live in North America now but we love Pee Yan Vee Yah.

But you work for us—for Canada, I say. Your a kind of police man. You have to serve and protect like it says on the cars.

Do you care about your country Bunny? he asks. What if Canada was in chains? Wuldnt you work to make it free?

Chains? I say.

Thats what the SPCA is about, he says.

At the customs place he dint know about the SPCA but now he does. He tells me what the letters stand for—something about Saving Pee Yan Vee Yah and a counter army. I dont get it. I dont get any of this.

No but—chains? I say.

Wuldnt you want the world to know your story? he asks. Wuldnt you want Aiden Tween to sing your national anthem? That is happening at city hall. That is why you must speak to your brother he says.

His face is long and his eyes are dark and hooded. It is totally weerd—he is walking me across a field of escaped cows talking about Aiden Tween and a counter army and chains around a place I never herd of until this week. Behind us Vi and Lubor are lying on the ice. Maybe they love Pee Yan Vee Yah as much as Joe does. Maybe Joe is hurt rite now. Maybe he was hit on the head and is a bit crazy.

Cows eh? Didnt I say they were mean?

The sky over the lake xplodes. Theres a ball of red and gold stars. Fireworks. It must be New Years. Joe is surprised enuff to look up and stumble and lose his balance. I take my chance and push. He stumbles some more. I push again and he falls to the ground.

The field has lousy ice but skating is still faster than walking. I take off. The cows are ahead of me and I go around them. Joe scrambles to his feet and tries to cut me off but he skids into a cow and she kicks him in the side. He falls. The cows gallop away.

A blu and green lite hangs in the sky and then a brite white comet type thing fizzles up and dies. I hear a clap of thunder. A shower of yellowy stars rains on us.

Joe is down. Vi and Lubor are still down. There is nobody moving around but me and the cows. They are clumped together by the big truck. I skate to the edge of the field near the CNE gates and hop onto the road. I know what to do now. I get out the phone and call a number from memory.

HI THANKS FOR CALLING OTOOLE CENTRAL.

At the sound of the tone leave a message for Deb Jerry Bunny or Spencer and well get back to you Scouts honor. And dont forget to wonder whats so crazy about peace love and understanding.

Dads voice. I hang up and call the other number I know. Jade ansers rite away. It sounds like there is a party in the background. When I say who I am the party sounds go away and it is just Jades voice.

Where are you Bunny? I dont know this phone number.

I explain what is going on—some of it. And where I am and what I want. Jade promises to help.

I know somebody who can get there in 10 minits. Look for a taxi.

I dont have any money for a taxi I say.

Dont worry about that—Herb will help anyone from the possy says Jade.

The firework show is finishing up. Spears of gold shoot up to the sky. Balls of fire explode into blu and green and red and orange flower petals that float down and disappear while claps and barks echo and fade. In the distance I hear the first of the sirens. The police are coming.

HERB DOESNT BELIEVE WHO I AM RITE AWAY

but when I unzip my coat and pull up my shirt sleeve to show him my 15 Street tatoo he lets me into the cab.

Man you dont look like you belong he says.

I know.

Jade says to come down to the Princes Gates and pick up 1 of the possy I am not looking for you he says.

I know.

Herb drives off without any more questions. He doesnt ask about the cows or the sirens or anything. If I am in the possy I am okay. For the first time in days I feel power full. The hole possy is behind me —Jade and Cobra and Scratch and Snocone and X-Ray and now Herb. His hair stands up like black fingers on his head. He wears driving gloves that fit tite. The cab smells spicy. We go along the lake and then up a hill into the city. When we meet the ambulances Herb pulls over to let them past. He pulls over again when we meet the police cars and the fire truck. I ask Herb how he is doing tonite and he says fine.

Spencer is not at city hall. The concert is over and the big square is almost empty. Its late and outside and the middle of winter. There is a stage off to the side and posters of Aiden Tween are flapping in the wind. Even from a distance I can see the capital letters. AT. The clock in the tall tower across the street bongs the time. 1 bong—1 oclock.

I dont know what to do so I go back to the cab witch is waiting by the curb. Herb reaches to the seat beside him and hands me a bag.

This is for you he says. Jade told me youd need them.

What? I say.

There my brothers he says. He wore them last year but hes 2 big for them now.

In the bag theres a pair of running shoes.

Jade said to get you a pair of shoes and go pick you up says Herb.

Wow I say.

Thats all. Wow. I dont know what else to say. Its thank you and you didnt have to and holy crap all at once. Herb waves it away.

My feet are recked. Wrecked. Ive been wearing rental skates all week. Now Im back where I rented them. I left my boots under a bench—theyll be long gone. I want to put on the runners—but not quite yet.

Wait another minit I tell Herb. This rink is still open. Can you wait a minit?

Your 15 he says. I do what you tell me. You want me to wait I wait. You want to drive to Vancoover I do that.

What?

Take a few days but I can do it.

Hes serious.

OK then give me a minit I say.

I hop my way over to the rink and do a lap. Push. Glide. Push. The ice is pretty good but my skates are so dull I slip a lot. I feel like crying but I cant do it. My chest heaves in and out but what comes out is a laff. Maybe I am 2 tired to cry and when you cant cry you laff insted. Its been a long week.

The Aiden Tween song playing on the sound system stops in the middle. *Hey you dancing in the corner by yourself dont look so sad its not so* —the lites go out 1 by 1. Now the rink is in darkness. An old guy comes out of the rental place. I go over and hand him my skates. He takes them and looks at them a long time.

These he says. Number 13.

Yeah.

These been gone for days he says. Where you find them?

On my feet.

What?

I turn away.

Wait a minit he says. But I am already gone in my new runners witch fit ok. A little long maybe but way better than socks. And maybe I will grow into them.

HERB IS LISTENING TO THE NEWS ON THE CAR RADIO

and shaking his head.

Crazy! he says.

What is?

What they say about the accident with all the cows he says.

We head along Queen Street. I take out the phone I have been using—the 1 from the front porch—and once again it doesnt work. I wonder if it is frozen? I had it in my outside coat pocket again. Maybe that was the problem befor.

I give Herb my address on Tecumseth. My home address. I can see it in my mind written out on an envelope cause I send a letter home every week. I dont know if anyone is there or not. Would Herb drive me to Creekside now if I asked? Would I ask?

I recognize all the stores we pass. Traffic is lite.

Whats that about the accident? I say.

Herb says something I dont catch xept for the last word.

Wolf? I say.

What the truck driver told the police says Herb. Says he saw this wolf run up from the lake and cross the lakeshore road rite in front of him. He jammed on the brakes so he wuldnt run into it. The truck skidded and crashed and the cows got out. Drivers fine but the truck and 2 cars are a mess and 3 people are in hospital. And all because of a wolf.

I cant help myself. I start laffing again. Is it as easy as that—is Grampa looking after me? Is that how I got home? Cause if its that easy why am I so tired? We turn down our street.

Herb looks at me like—Whats so funny? But he doesnt ask any questions.

Theres a lite in an upstares window at my place. I see a shadow for a second and then its gone.

Herb holds up a box of kleenex he keeps on the dash. I take a few.

Thanks I say. My voice cracks and I try again. Thanks.

I wipe away the tears.

ACKNOWLEDGMENTS

A book is a team effort—writer, muse, agent, editorial, sales and marketing, publicity, to say nothing of friends and family and so on. But the Seven series has been a team effort from the writing point of view as well. I am deeply grateful to all my co-authors, certainly Eric Walters for providing the initial spark, but also and especially to Ted Staunton for his great work on our goofy interwoven plots. A lot of the success of the series has been author driven. Guys and Norah, it has been a pleasure to hang out with you across Canada this past year, and I look forward to doing it again. And let's not forget the Orca publishing team—Andrew, Sarah, Dayle and all the others who didn't buy me dinner, who didn't check my spelling eleven million times and whose shower I did not break. Thank you.

RICHARD SCRIMGER is the award-winning author of twenty books for children and adults. His middle-school novel *The Nose from Jupiter* won the Mr. Christie's Award, and his books have appeared on the *Globe and Mail*'s and ALA's notable-books lists. His books have been translated into almost a dozen languages (actually, eleven). The father of four, Richard is used to being laughed at. *The Wolf and Me* is the sequel to *Ink Me*, Richard's novel in Seven (the series).

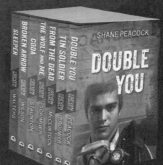

ONE

TORONTO: DECEMBER 27

Bunny's gone. I stepped off the ice to get us sausages from the truck, which *he* wanted (my brother doesn't get street meat these days), and now, when I turn back, he's vanished.

What's with that? I hoover a sausage and scope the place. I saw the latest James Bond movie before Christmas, and I've been doing his laser stare ever since. I think I rock it, even with glasses. Q should be talking in my earbud.

The rink at city hall is hopping tonight: skaters in bright colors, Christmas decorations, tinny music, cold. At the far side, the scaffolding is set up for the New

Year's Eve concert stage. This year it's Aiden Tween. Since I'm not a twelve-year-old girl, I plan to miss it. Meanwhile, the hiss of blades on ice reminds me of the Komodo dragons Bond escaped from in *Skyfall*. I whip out my phone and grab a few seconds of video. I imagine an overhead shot, patterns of people flowing, Bond zipping through them. Hey, a chase scene on ice! I bet no one's ever done it. I could use Bunny—he's a good skater.

But Bunny's not skating. Maybe he's hit the washroom. Before I check, I take time to polish off his sausage too. I guess I'm hungrier than I thought. Besides, Bunny's not the only person I'm looking for. I haven't seen AmberLea since September, and it might be nice to meet her on my own.

I don't see AmberLea either. I fire Bun a text—where r u—then AmberLea: skating remember? I turn to look for Bunny near the sausage truck and hear my ringtone, those eerie first notes from *The Good, the Bad and the Ugly*. I dig out my phone again. AmberLea has texted: pan 180. I get it; AmberLea is in first-year film school, like me. I turn around and there she is, on the ice right behind me.

"Hey!" I say.

"Spencer!" It's not Oscar-quality dialogue, but I'll take it. AmberLea's arms are stretched out. Is this for a hello hug or just for balance? Should I go for the hug? What if it's a bad call? I solve the problem by forgetting I'm wearing skates as I step forward. I stumble onto the ice and practically land on top of her.

"Whoa!" She helps me stand up. "Hey, new glasses. Like 'em."

I fumble them back into place. I've replaced my wire frames with clunky black ones, which are very cool right now. Plus, they go with the old curling sweater I found in a vintage store, decorated with crossed brooms and deer antlers. I am now urban cool. AmberLea says, "There's mustard on your chin."

"What? Oh, sorry." I swipe at my chin. So much for cool.

"No problem." She gives me a real hug. AmberLea looks great, as usual. Her blond hair sweeps out from under the same kind of hat Dad got Bunny and me for Christmas. I instantly revise my opinion on wooly yellow-and-blue hats with earflaps and tie strings. Maybe I'll wear mine after all. I see she has matching mittens too. All in all, AmberLea makes a great picture—until someone else barges into the frame. A big guy showers me with ice flakes in a perfect hockey stop. "This is Toby," AmberLea says. "We're friends at school."

"Hey," says Toby. He's wearing the same hat. I re-revise my opinion and make a mental note to give my hat to the first street person I see. Underneath the hat, Toby has a perfect swoop of brown hair and a perfect, stubbly face above a perfect suede bomber jacket with a perfect long, preppy scarf that matches the hat. I know his skates are expensive, because Bunny has the same kind. I hate him already.

I shake hands with Toby (who does *that*?), trying for my best manly man grip. He says, "AmberLea's told me about you," in some kind of clipped American accent. I wonder which parts she told him.

"She was probably just kidding," I say.

Toby laughs. That doesn't help.

"So," AmberLea says, "let's skate." Uh-oh. I was so anxious to see AmberLea, I never thought about the actual skating part. The only ice I can handle is in a glass of Scotch—and that's not even my line; it's from a movie about a killer glacier. I don't even drink Scotch.

"Um," I say, "actually, I have to look for Bunny."

They both look surprised. How much has AmberLea told this guy? "Bunny?" AmberLea says. "Isn't he…?"

I nod. "But he's home for Christmas. It's complicated. He was with me and now he's gone, and he's only supposed to be with family, so I have to find him."

"Can we help?" Toby asks.

"Naw, it's okay. You skate. He's probably just in the washroom. When I find him, we'll come back." Or maybe not. Maybe I'll just go somewhere and die.

"Where are the washrooms?" says AmberLea.

"Over there." I point to the far end of the rink.

"C'mon, we'll skate over with you."

"Oh, that's okay."

"*C'mon.*" AmberLea beckons and does a nifty little backup glide.

Oh, man. What can I do? "Bloody hell," I whisper in my best Brit accent. *Man up, Bond.* Right. Notice James Bond never skates? I push off carefully. Except for falling over, wobbling forward is all I can do on skates. I keep my hands out, legs spread wide enough to drive the sausage truck between them. I'm swearing in a steady stream under my breath.

This is Bun's fault. He's the one who wanted to

skate. He'd even wanted to skate on the lake up at Grandpa's cottage yesterday if the ice was strong enough. Then all the crazy stuff happened, and we forgot about it. As soon as we got home today, Bunny said, "Come on, Spence. My only chance, maybe."

I was good with it. AmberLea and her mom were in town, staying at the hotel across the street from city hall. I texted her, figuring we'd sit on a bench and talk while Bun skated. I really wanted to tell her about what had happened at the cottage. Besides, I felt kind of sorry for Bun. He's not exactly having fun these days.

Now I'm not having fun, and AmberLea and Toby are politely pretending not to notice. Toby is skating backward, which does not make me like him any better. My exit is coming up. If I glide now, I should run out of gas as my toes bump the end of the rink. This is good, because I don't know how to stop either.

AmberLea and Toby start their turn. I don't. "Back in a bit," I call. AmberLea waves. My toes kiss the edge of the rink.